"Sometimes I wish that things had been different."

"Sometimes I do too."

She turned away from the telescope and looked at Jordan. Her skin was luminous and her eyes shiny in the dark. She had never been more beautiful.

"What else do you wish for?" His fingers found the narrow hollow of her spine. He could feel her trembling, but she did not pull away.

Her gaze dropped to his cravat, flickered to his face, then back to his cravat again. "There was a time . . ." she began.

She was talking about the night at the opera. The night when he had kissed her. He brought his fingers under her chin and forced her to look at him. "Is that what you wish for?"

"Oh, you don't even know what I was going to say." She gave an embarrassed laugh and tried to move away, but he kept her close.

"I counted three hundred falling stars last night," he whispered. "And with every one I wished to kiss you."

She looked confused, and even in the dark he could tell that she was blushing. "Don't be ridiculous, Jordan," she chided. "Besides"—she gave a tiny nervous laugh—"doling out three hundred kisses would take ages."

"What do you wish for Phoebe?" he asked again.

They looked at each other for a moment, both unsure.

She rose onto her toes until she was eye to eye with him. "Let me show you." And then she leaned in and kissed him. . . .

Books by Catherine Blair

Published by Zebra Books

A
SCHOLARLY
GENTLEMAN

Catherine Blair

ZEBRA BOOKS
Kensington Publishing Corp.
http://www.kensingtonbooks.com

ZEBRA BOOKS are published by

Kensington Publishing Corp.
850 Third Avenue
New York, NY 10022

All Kensington titles, imprints, and distributed lines are available at special quantity discounts for bulk purchases for sales promotion, premiums, fund-raising, educational or institutional use.

Special book excerpts or customized printings can also be created to fit specific needs. For details, write or phone the office of the Kensington Special Sales Manager: Kensington Publishing Corp., 850 Third Avenue, New York, NY 10022. Attn. Special Sales Department. Phone: 1-800-221-2647.

First Printing: August 2002
10 9 8 7 6 5 4 3 2 1

Printed in the United States of America

One

The heavy iron-bound door was opened with such force that it crashed against the wall. Two-dozen robed students in the silent dining hall looked up and stared at the woman framed dramatically in the doorway.

"Well," she said, her glittering eyes expectant and cold, "I have come."

Professor Jordan Blakely DeVaux looked up from his beef. "So I see." He watched impassively from the high table as the two frightened-looking porters wrestled a mountain of trunks into the hall, then he went back to eating, unwilling to let the whole of Trinity College see that he was furious.

Whispers blew up and down the ranks of tables as the students speculated on the sudden appearance of the tall, fair goddess wearing a defiant scowl. No one had ever walked in in the middle of hall. Certainly not a woman. It was unheard of.

"Professor Lord DeVaux," the master hissed, evidently having discovered the intruder's connection by following the line of her glare. "Who is this lady? And what the devil does she think she's doing barging in here?" Obviously he recognized that she was an important-enough personage that she couldn't be reprimanded directly.

Jordan sighed. "She is my cousin's widow, sir. She has come up from London to live in Cambridge with my sister and her husband."

"Professor *Lord* DeVaux has thrown me out of my house," the woman announced. He noted that she put special emphasis on the title he had inherited upon her husband's death.

Another wave of murmurs swept through the undergraduates.

Of course they had heard that Professor DeVaux had inherited the vicountancy when his cousin died last year, but they hadn't known that his widow was a beautiful woman with hate gleaming in her remarkably green eyes. It lent itself all too deliciously to scandal.

The master's expression, however, was none too pleased. After bestowing DeVaux with a look of extreme censure, he turned to the woman, who still stood silhouetted in the doorway. "Madam—"

"Please remove Lady DeVaux's luggage from the dining hall," Jordan said to the head porter. That man darted a nervous glance at Lady DeVaux, and wiped the sweat beading on his forehead. He had good reason to be worried; the lady had drawn herself up tight as a bowstring. "You may put her trunks in my chambers for the time being," Jordan continued, ignoring her look of chagrin. "Inform Lady DeVaux that if she will be kind enough to await me there, I will attend her when dinner is over."

That would pique her of course. Grand Lady DeVaux from London having to await him like a tradesman. Well it would serve her right for her melodramatic entrance.

The porters obediently shuffled out with her trunks, carefully maneuvering a wide berth around the woman as she stood with her arms crossed tightly over her fashionable fur-edged spencer. Jordan thought for a moment that she would refuse to go. But the wide eyes and gaping mouths of the undergraduates must have reminded her of her dignity, and she contented herself with giving him a look of loathing over her shoulder as she stalked from the room.

At his elbow, Professor Caldwell unsuccessfully stifled a laugh. "Relations!" he exclaimed, digging back into his meal. "Always descending upon you when they're least wanted." He waggled his brows and grinned. "And the pretty ones are always the harridans."

Jordan went back to eating. He'd no real appetite now, but he would be damned if he'd show that she'd embarrassed him. "Oh, my late cousin's wife is descending at my behest," he said quietly. "I've had to let the London town house, and she is to live with my sister until we can make other arrangements. I shouldn't like to see Hillary's face when she sees that woman has brought seven trunks full of ridiculously expensive clothes."

"I'm sure she'll wear them well," the fellow Trinity professor mused. "She's a diamond of the first water, to be sure. It's been a long time since I've seen a woman of fashion." He grinned again, this time with more devilment. "If you can keep her from acting like Mrs. Siddons all the time, I might drop over to your sister's for tea."

DeVaux said nothing, concentrating solely on

keeping every expression from his face. He'd known, of course, that she would come. She had no choice. He had anticipated a scene, particularly after the angry letters they'd exchanged over her right to use the town house now that he'd inherited the title. He hadn't expected her to flounce right into the college dining hall and perform her histrionics in front of the students, but he likely should have.

The woman was nothing but a spoiled child.

"Of course," Caldwell continued, "females who aren't related don't tend to live well together. Particularly when both are used to running their own households. We had fireworks when my father's sister moved in with us. Now, I know your sister is a most sweet-tempered creature, but your new guest—" He trailed off ominously.

"—is likely to make all of our lives hell," DeVaux finished.

She'd lived a life of privilege since she'd come into this world and her marriage to Arthur had secured her position as a luminary of the *beau monde*. In the eight years of their marriage, Lord and Lady DeVaux had managed to gamble their way through her dowry, his fortune, and several other people's fortunes besides.

They lived their lives in separate realms as expected in the upper circles but somehow managed to run through twice as much money that way. Charming, beautiful, profligate wastrels, both of them. No one had been terribly surprised that Arthur DeVaux had ended up on Primrose Hill with a bullet from a dueling pistol in his head. Jordan hadn't heard the details; university men kept their heads in their books and their noses out of other people's business. Which was likely for the best, as the less one knew of *ton* affairs, the better.

He'd been very close to his cousin at one time. Inseparable. There was something impossible not to like about the man. Even later, years later, when they'd parted ways, Jordan to follow more serious pursuits, Arthur to chase wilder ones, he still missed his cousin's company.

But Arthur was dead now. Dead for over a year, if Lady DeVaux's fashionable state of half mourning was any indication. And now, once again, Jordan would step in to pick up the pieces Arthur had left behind.

He heard the master's chair scrape back and stood up along with the rest of those seated at the high table. The students followed suit and waited while the fellows made their formal recessional from the room. Jordan could virtually hear the speculation whirring around in their little heads. He kept his eyes on Caldwell's back.

Outside, most of the fellows ambled off toward the combination room, likely to spin out their own speculations over glasses of port. DeVaux half expected to see Arthur's wife fuming in the hallway outside the dining hall. But there was no sign of her or her mountain of trunks. She could have gone straight to Hillary's house, of course, but he doubted she would leave the premises without giving him a rather large piece of her mind.

He walked across the lawn to his own rooms, pretending that his head wasn't hammering and that this had been a good decision. It was Hillary and her husband who would have to suffer Lady DeVaux, after all. They were the ones who had agreed to take the woman in. He himself would not be expected to have anything to do with her. Once this unpleasant interview was over, she would be as invisible as if she had stayed in the damned house in London.

An unnatural darkness at the top of the stairs confirmed his suspicions. There was a stack of trunks blocking the light from the hall window outside of his chambers. Lady DeVaux was there, too, alone. She didn't look quite so fierce at the moment. Her hands were clasped together in an attitude of deep thought, her frame slumped slightly against the trunks. She'd taken off her bonnet, and the bright gold of her bowed head made a strange light note in the tableau.

She looked up at the sound of his approach and the mask of coldness descended.

"Lord DeVaux," she said, managing in the two words to imply it was his fault that he'd inherited the title from Arthur. "Or rather Professor Lord DeVaux. How lofty that sounds. Who would have expected you to end up a university professor? Math is it?"

From someone else it would be teasing, arch even, but from her it sounded insulting. "I teach astronomy," he corrected her. They stood for a moment in the hallway, not speaking. Finally he conceded defeat and dug in his pocket for the key to his chambers.

She entered, holding her skirts close to keep them from touching him. He caught the scent she wore as she passed and felt a wave of some vague, disquieting emotion. He followed her in and shut the door.

"Small," she said, looking around the rooms. A

tiny wrinkle formed between the fine arches of her brows. "I would have thought a grand Cambridge fellow like you would have something more expansive."

"My needs are few," he said brusquely. Though he looked around, critical for the first time in years, and saw that the bedder had not properly dusted the bookshelf and that the curtains in the window were badly faded from the sun. Perhaps he should have hung a picture on the wall or some such frippery.

She evidently had come to the conclusion that he was not going to ask her to sit, so she sat down anyway. The faint look of curiosity she had worn briefly upon entering his chambers was replaced again with the inexpressively cool one.

They stared at each other in charged, hostile silence. The only sound in the room was that of a large bluebottle fly beating itself to death against the window.

"It has been a long time, Phoebe."

Her mouth moved, but he could not tell if it was a smile. "Nearly nine years."

The memories dislodged and fell upon him like an avalanche. God, how he'd wanted her. He'd been wild about her. Obsessed. In love. Or at least he'd thought himself to be.

"That long?" Though of course he knew exactly how long it had been.

She closed her eyes and drew a breath. When she opened them, the full force of her clear gaze was upon him. "Why did you force me to come here, Jordan?"

He stiffened, drawing himself back to the present.

That time long ago was not to be contemplated. Nine years ago she'd chosen Arthur. Not him. "We've discussed this many times in our correspondence."

He was tempted for a moment to sit down, but decided it was safer to stand. Sitting there, knee to knee, it would be too intimate. Even this barren, scruffy little room was too intimate. There likely had never been a woman in these chambers before, besides the bedders. At least not during his tenure, anyway. The setting sun slanted across the court, too bright to look at, but he resisted drawing the blinds. Too intimate.

"Lord and Lady Ramsbottom have rented the London house for the Season and will take up residence next week."

She looked wounded. "But—"

"I need not remind you that the town house is now mine. I fail to see why you are so sentimental about it. If it had not been entailed along with the rest of the property, you would happily have gambled it away like everything else."

Her lower lip dropped slightly as though she were going to protest, then was stilled between her teeth. Her eyes narrowed.

Jordan summoned up his resolve. Yes, at first he had been struck by her beauty, by the fact that she looked exactly the same as she had nine years ago. For a moment, he had seen only the young Miss Phoebe Grantham who had come to London for her first season and taken the town by storm.

How old was she now? Twenty-seven? She hardly looked it. Her face was thinner, perhaps, but it suited her. It emphasized her cheekbones and full lips. Her brows still rose in a graceful arch with the tiny mole, like a grace note, above the left. She still had that habit of gesturing with her hands when she talked. She still could make a man lose all powers of higher reasoning.

In nine years of hard and fast living, she had managed to retain that guileless look, that radiance, that compellingly sensual innocence. But of course it was only an illusion.

"I did not care to have you running up bills in London that I would have to pay," he continued, when she did not speak.

Her eyes were burning into him, the momentary softness he had seen vaporized by resentment. "Did you know you owed your milliner two hundred pounds?" he asked calmly.

The resentment burst into surprise. "That much?"

"I collect you had neglected to pay her for the last four years. There was also the matter of the town phaeton, the pair of bays, the shoemaker. . . . How can a woman buy twenty-three pairs of shoes in one year when she has only two feet? And the wine merchant."

Her chin rose, as though she were trying to keep it above the heated flush that crept up her neck. "Arthur said he'd taken care of those."

The bills had dated before her husband's death, that was true enough. But was the creature such a widgeon that she hadn't noted that the dunning notices kept coming?

"I paid the servants," she whispered, her chin still high, "and the rest of the housekeeping expenses after . . . after he died."

She looked so frail. For a moment he felt guilty

about speaking so harshly to her. After all, he'd allowed things to get to this state. If she was a spendthrift, perhaps it was partly his fault. He hadn't been able to bring himself to check in on her until now. For months he had avoided the issue, hoping somehow that the title, the responsibilities, Phoebe herself, would not ever manage to penetrate his intellectual seclusion.

She'd been left very much to fend for herself. He had sent his man of business to take care of the will. He'd been too much of a coward to contemplate seeing her himself.

He hadn't seen her since the funeral. And even then, they'd allowed the buffer of friends and family to keep them from meeting. He'd shaken her hand, murmured a few disjointed words of condolence, and gone to sit in Arthur's billiard room alone. At the time, he'd been too shocked by Arthur's death to think much about anything. Arthur, who could win everything from you and still leave you laughing. Gone.

But now Arthur's destitute wife was sitting here before him in his shabby little sitting room looking surprised to know that debts didn't go away if one didn't pay them.

He sat down across from her, reached for her hands, then recalled what he was doing. He pressed his fingertips together instead, as though he were lecturing. "I think it would be better if you were to live with Hillary and her husband for a little while. You will like Hillary, and she is anxious to have you."

He started to go on and explain the myriad advantages of living on charity with a stranger and her husband when she looked up at him, an expression of pain beneath her defiant look. "Are you punishing me, Jordan?"

He felt another needling of conscience. Was he? "Of course not," he said with a laugh, unwilling to examine his feelings further. "I have brought you here because I can no longer afford to let you run rampant in London." He said it lightly though, inexplicably hoping to see the tight worry in her face relax. "Besides," he added, "now that Arthur is gone, you should be with your family."

She rose to her feet. Perhaps it was only the dark trim to her gray gown or a trick of the evening light, but she looked paler than he'd remembered. And tired.

"You know well enough that I have no family of my own to go to," she said quietly. "I will stay in Cambridge as you wish, but only until I can save enough money to pay you back."

"Don't be ridiculous, Phoebe. There's no need—"

"I will repay my debts, and I will go back to London. I've lived far too long letting other people make my decisions for me. Papa, Arthur, you . . . I've lived my whole life just floating along and going with the current. No more. I will stay with your sister, but it is only temporary."

She straightened her shoulders, and he could see now that in the years since they had met, her face had taken on a new expression of strained resolution. "You hold the purse strings at the moment; you hold all the cards. But I will live here in Cambridge, upon your charity, not one moment longer that I have to." She leveled that green gaze at him. "I will do whatever it takes to become self-sufficient."

He'd done the right thing in bringing her here. He'd not really had a choice, given her debt. But he wondered now, as he looked into her face filled with fierce determination, if his quiet, ordered little life was about to be turned on end.

Two

Arthur was dead. For the first time since his death, Phoebe truly felt the weight of it. She looked around the cheerful little room decorated in yellow chintz, with its braided rug covering the worn spot in front of the door and the silver slightly freckled around the edges of the mirror above the washstand. Unmoored from her own belongings and familiar surroundings, she suddenly felt very alone in the world.

In the town house on Curzon Street, she had lived in a strange state of permanent waiting. The funeral had come and gone, but it hadn't really seemed like Arthur's. She'd obediently donned widow's weeds and sat through the sympathy calls. But it had always seemed as though any moment Arthur would burst through the door, shouting for a drink and laughing his head off at the grand joke he'd played on everyone. She couldn't even really say that she'd missed him, because he didn't really seem gone.

Now, however, in this cozy little room that would be her new home, she felt a strange, empty sense of loss. Arthur was dead. Things would never be the same.

She would have preferred to have sat for a while and indulged in a bit of self-pity, but the maid scratched at the door and then looked with dismay at the pile of trunks. "You've a lot of clothes, ma'am," she said in a voice between awe and disapproval.

"I know. I didn't have anywhere to store them since the town house was let." It was a weak excuse, really, even if true enough. She didn't know why she should feel compelled to apologize, when most of the ladies she knew had at least as many gowns. She thought of Jordan DeVaux's look of stony disapproval and reminded herself that she didn't care what anyone thought in this provincial little town.

"Good heavens, milady!" the girl exclaimed, coming up from her rummage holding a gown lavishly trimmed in jet. "I've never seen the like."

Phoebe turned back from the mirror to see that the maid had festooned the room with rich clothes. In the plain little house they looked gaudy. "You can put it away, Annie. I won't be wearing it here."

Annie surreptitiously held the dress up to herself to check the fit. Phoebe wondered what her old dresser Saunders would have thought of Annie's cheeky good humor. But she'd had to let Saunders go with the rest of the London servants.

If Jordan wanted her to be a poor relation, so be it. She had come with nothing but her pride and her personal belongings. And after hearing how much she'd run into debt, she had very little left to be proud of.

She stood up and shook out her skirts. Very well, enough moping. She'd had plenty of time to freshen up, and to wait longer to go downstairs to the Hartfields would be rude. How odd to think that she would be spending every evening with these strangers-turned-relations from now on. Until she found a way to pay off those horrid debts. "Do you know Lord DeVaux?" she asked the girl. "Professor DeVaux, I mean."

Annie smiled. "Of course, milady."

"And what do you think of him?" It was a stupid question; the girl's eyes were bright with adoration already.

Annie crushed a Belgian lace ball gown to her bosom. "He's so very kind. Not that he often speaks to me, mind. But he always remembers my name. And he made Mrs. Hartfield let me have the day off when I had a toothache. And he's teaching my brother George to write his letters, and he's always—"

"A paragon," Phoebe interrupted dryly.

"I wouldn't be able to say about that, ma'am." Annie looked doubtful. "I don't have a head for numbers. But Professor DeVaux is everything clever. I'm sure I don't understand half what he says."

Phoebe laughed. "You don't understand what a dog says either. But you don't think he's clever."

The maid looked rather struck by this notion. "Well, milady," she said, diving back into the trunk, "I wouldn't be able to say about that. I know some very clever dogs."

Phoebe went down the stairs feeling somewhat cheered. Her time in Cambridge could be interesting. After all, she hadn't left London since she'd married. Arthur couldn't abide the country, so they never went further than house parties in Richmond. Of course she would miss the Season, but there was little loss in that. Things had grown quite flat in

Town, and the last few years it had seemed as though every Season was like the last.

It certainly hadn't been her wish to come here, but perhaps Jordan's idea wasn't so terrible after all. As long as Jordan himself kept his distance. She didn't wish to admit it, but she'd been shaken by her interview with him. It stirred up memories and feelings she thought were long put to rest.

The Hartfields were sitting by the fire, the picture of domestic bliss. Mr. Hartfield sat with the paper in front of his face while his wife was engaged in rapt conversation with the infant on her knee.

"Lady DeVaux, how lovely you look," Mrs. Hartfield exclaimed. "Isn't she a picture, my lamb? I'm afraid she puts us all in the shade."

Phoebe was not certain if the woman was addressing her husband or the child, since both of them merely stared at her and made no response. Compared to her hostess's simple round gown, her own lace-trimmed creation looked very overworked.

"I'm afraid I don't have anything appropriate for the country," she said, feeling a little foolish.

She'd had little opportunity to observe Mrs. Hartfield when she first arrived at the house. Now she could see that she resembled her brother strongly indeed. Her face was rounder, full of plump good nature, and her hair a redder brown, but they both had the same deep-set dark eyes, generous mouth, and peculiar way of tipping their head to the side when they talked.

Mrs. Hartfield deposited her child with the nursery maid and went to Phoebe. "I'm certain you're used to things being very grand. How trying it must be. But I do hope you'll be more comfortable with family than you were rattling around that old house all alone. I'm so glad Jordan made you accept our invitation. It will be so cheerful now that you're here, don't you think, Hartfield?" She gave a breathy laugh and looked at her husband, who lowered his paper only long enough to mutter some kind of greeting before diving back into its folds. Phoebe had a brief impression of a stocky man with enormous mustaches before he disappeared.

"Now come and sit here by the fire, dearest Lady DeVaux. Did you eat the dinner I sent up to you? I know it can't be what you're used to, but I hope you did eat it. You're far too thin. But don't despair, Cook is very good at tempting even the most fussy appetite. Baby won't eat a thing unless Cook makes it special."

"Yes, I ate, and it was very good. I certainly hope you don't think I expect a tray in my room all the time. You shall quite spoil me."

"We'd eaten already when you arrived," said Mr. Hartfield, unexpectedly surfacing again. "Country hours." He stared hard at her. "Though you know"—he gave great weight to the words—"that Cambridge is a town. Not the country." He regarded her rather severely over the top of the newspaper.

"Certainly. The buildings of the university are quite grand."

"Pooh. The university. Cambridge is more than just the university. Though you wouldn't know it to hear some of the dons there," he said, his mustaches aquiver with annoyance. "Even without the students, Cambridge is a respectably sized town. We have more bookshops than Bath, you know. And our own right to print books as well. Can't say that about most towns."

"I daresay Lady DeVaux doesn't care about such things," Mrs. Hartfield said quickly. She shot Phoebe a smile that reminded her of Jordan. Back in the days when Jordan used to smile.

"Please call me Phoebe. After all, we are cousins through marriage. And we certainly shouldn't stand on ceremony when you are being so kind to me." She tried not to uncharitably call to mind that they would not have been forced to take her in if Jordan had not evicted her.

Mrs. Hartfield looked relieved. "And you should call me Hillary. I must say, I'm so glad to find that you aren't too high in the instep. We'd heard—well that is, some people are, you know."

Had she really come across that way? She thought of her dramatic entrance at Trinity and cringed.

"We shall be the very best of friends," Hillary continued. "Mrs. Lane is quite anxious to meet you. Why, the whole town is expecting you. We don't often get grand ladies down from London.

"We shall have to go on a great many morning calls right away so I can introduce you to everyone," she went on. "Now you mustn't mind if Celia Worth stares at you, she does it to everyone and it's only because she's shortsighted." She stopped in the middle of her prattle and beamed. "I cannot think why Jordan did not bring you down before. It will be such fun to have you here."

A thought suddenly struck Phoebe. "It seems very strange that we never met before. Did you not ever go to London? It seems odd that Arthur would not have introduced us years ago."

Hillary and her husband exchanged glances. "We have been to London many times. We took the most darling little house in Holborn for a month during the Season last year." She looked suddenly stricken. "We should have called, I know. But we—" She hesitated. "We were not close to Arthur."

Phoebe thought back. Had she met any of her husband's relations besides Jordan? Of course there had been many at the funeral, but before? At the beginning?

She had avoided the memory of that spring for so long that it was hard to chase it down. It was her first Season, the Season she'd met the DeVaux cousins. And Jordan and Arthur had been inseparable. The memory of the day she had first met them seemed so long ago, she wondered if she'd embellished it beyond recognition in her mind.

Jordan and Arthur had been riding together in the park, alike as two peas. Both were tall and athletic, with unruly dark hair and laughing brown eyes. Jordan was the taller, and at the time she'd thought him the handsomer, the more clever, the more kind. She shook off the thought. That was a long time ago.

Relations, yes, she was trying to recall relations. Had she met anyone else? His mother of course. She doted upon her only son and could find no fault with him. Her death had prostrated Arthur. His father had died long before she'd even met her future husband. She tried to remember the rest of his family. Had she and Arthur really been so isolated?

"Though we were very sorry to hear of Arthur's untimely death," Hillary added, very belatedly.

"Yes," Phoebe said, feeling a stab of regret. "So

unexpected. One never expects anyone to die in a duel. I didn't even know he knew Lord Whitcombe."

Jordan's sister glanced at her husband, who was once again entrenched behind the news, and drew her chair closer. "We read that it was Whitcombe who killed him," she said in a low voice. "What became of him?"

It was strange to talk of it. Phoebe had told the story many times before, but that had been just after it had happened. Before was real. It seemed harder to speak of his death now. "Lord Whitcombe went to the Continent after the duel. I'm not certain where. France, I heard." She felt her throat tightening and her eyes prickle with emotions she did not wish to feel. "He was never brought to trial." She sighed and then attempted a laugh. "Ah well, I read that Whitcombe died in Brussels last summer. Drank himself to death. All for a stupid disagreement. I cannot believe that men are so barbarous."

The paper rattled ominously but remained upright.

Hillary's eyes were wide. "And Lady Whitcombe?"

"She did not go with him. I believe they had lived apart for years." She thought back to those dark days after Arthur died. They seemed a long time ago. But her future stretched out even longer ahead of her.

Hillary nodded as though she had heard that as well. Her voice dropped. "So she could remarry now, couldn't she? That poor woman."

Phoebe felt suddenly tired. Two men had a petty, drunken disagreement and as a result so many lives were ruined.

Yes, poor Lady Whitcombe. Frankly she had disliked the woman for many reasons. But she had never really given Lady Whitcombe's husband any thought at all. How strange that she should have met Lord Whitcombe at any number of parties and balls and never guessed that he would play such an important role in her future.

"Ah, here's Annie with the tea tray. And Jordan!" Hillary jumped up and went to embrace her brother. "You naughty man, why didn't you knock? Skulking about here like a thief. Come in and have some tea. Have you dined? Of course you have. But have you dined well? Cook will have some cold victuals if you are still hungry."

It was strange to see the change in Hillary as she clung to her brother's sleeve. Did everyone worship the man? Phoebe felt her own heart beating harder as she steeled herself for battle. He must not see how he affected her, how he still held some strange power over her from the past.

"Hello, DeVaux," said Hartfield, standing up and shaking his brother-in-law by the hand. "Haven't seen you in weeks. Busy at the college, eh? Can't see what you get out of spending your time trying to drum some knowledge into the wooden heads of noblemen. Just starting your day are you?"

"Oh, Jordan, you aren't are you?" exclaimed Hillary. "It can't be healthy to stay up all night. I know you must spend your time looking at the stars and all that, but starting one's day at dinnertime seems so, so . . . uncouth."

Jordan looked past his sister. "Lady DeVaux," he said in the same calm voice he'd used when they'd met in the college. He gave her a graceful bow better suited to a royal salon than the Hartfields' ordinary little drawing room. "Are you settling in?"

She suddenly found herself standing on trembling legs. "Yes. Thank you. I'm very happy here." Oh good God. Couldn't she think of anything better to say than that? Where was the anger she had used to hold herself together earlier? Then she had been so furious at him for forcing her out of her home that she had managed to forget, for a moment, how handsome he was.

Seeing him in his cap and gown was peculiar. He looked severe and scholarly, like a different person. But beneath it was still the man she had known. He looked older, perhaps. Graver certainly. The dark eyes that used to always be alight with humor, now looked reserved, even resigned. But they still looked down at her with an intensity that staggered her.

"Good," he said. "I knew Hillary would make you welcome."

Phoebe had the sudden suspicion that contrary to Jordan's letters, it had not been originally Hillary's idea that she should come live in Cambridge. But why in heaven's name would Jordan want to drag her out here? They hadn't spoken since . . . since a long time ago.

"Where are you off to tonight?" Hartfield asked, folding the paper with obvious regret.

"I have my regular Wednesday night lecture at the observatory at eleven," he replied, sitting down and stretching out his legs. "So I thought I would walk out toward Grantchester until then."

"But it's pitch dark. Not a sliver of moon. You'll likely fall in the Cam and drown."

Jordan grinned, and Phoebe realized it was the first time she had seen him really smile since she had arrived. "The moon is for poets. The stars are for astronomers."

"I find it so peculiar that you became a professor, Jordan," she said with a laugh. "Particularly of astronomy. I had no idea you were interested in it."

His smile was gone and the room felt suddenly cold. It was as though she'd started singing at the wrong time in church, or stood up and begun trying to converse with the actors on the stage.

"Well, a man must do something," he said with a half shrug.

Of course that wasn't true. Arthur was proof enough of that. A man with means needn't do anything. And Jordan had his own fortune. There was no reason he could not have stayed in London, living every day merely for its pleasure as Arthur had done. She admitted to herself that she had not wanted Jordan to stay in London. She had been glad when he left, but until now, she had not wondered why.

And how had he ended up here teaching astronomy?

Her interest was piqued. He'd been the picture of a London beau when she knew him. Intelligent, but certainly not scholarly. Why in heaven's name had he taken it into his head to come to Cambridge?

"May I come to your class?" she asked, before she even knew she'd thought it.

Everyone in the room stared at her.

"That would not be appropriate," Jordan said repressively when she continued to look at him with a questioning expression.

"Nonsense. I am a respectable widow. Certainly not some young miss. There can be no harm in it."

His dark eyes were unreadable. "You are not enrolled in the university. You can't just walk into lectures."

It was true. She'd been foolish to suggest it. It wouldn't be fair to the students. It was a serious course of study, not just something for people to walk in on on a whim. "I'm sorry. I was merely curious. I can't imagine you teaching. And astronomy of all things. Who would have thought it?"

"Yes. Who would have thought it from a gadabout like me," he echoed.

"You and Arthur never seemed serious about anything," she continued. She remembered Jordan's laugh so clearly. He had always been ready to see the ridiculousness of life. She'd never imagined he would end up swathed in black robes, grave as a Quaker.

Jordan suddenly became absorbed in stirring his tea. "There was one thing I was very serious about," he said quietly. He looked at her for a moment, then turned his eyes away.

Her heart was beating painfully hard within her. She gripped the arms of the chair and forced herself to smile blandly, as though she didn't understand exactly what he meant. Nine years was too long ago to harbor regrets. She would not let his words drag her back to the past.

"Well," she said with a careless shrug, "I won't scandalize the town by walking in on your lectures then. I shall be the most respectable widow in town." She could not resist tossing him a thin smile. "Even nine years ago, our little scandal was a nine-day wonder at best."

Jordan let the words hang in the air and then

come crashing down in the silence. "You mean when you broke our engagement in order to marry Arthur?" he said cuttingly at last. "Oh yes, that was forgotten long ago."

Three

"Professor DeVaux!"

The shout came down the empty road so loudly that Jordan could not conceivably pretend not to hear it.

"Professor DeVaux! How lucky that I came across you." Boxty Fuller came trotting out of the tavern, his long limbs flapping jointlessly.

"Hello, Fuller," Jordan said, bowing. The tall, thin boy looked more than half cut and was obviously anxious to talk. Even sober, his student was a chatterbox. Jordan suppressed a frown. He'd been looking forward to the solitary walk to Grantchester. He needed the time to think.

"Almost didn't see you in the dark, sir," Fuller said, drawing up beside him. He blew out his cheeks with an exaggerated expression of exertion, his normally florid color even more pronounced. The young man's flush was more likely from the heat or the wares of the tavern than the short jog across the road. "Was sitting in Crooks for a tipple or two with a few of the lads, and I said to Blinkers, why that's Professor DeVaux. No it ain't, said Blinkers. What would he be doing walking about in the middle of the night? It is Professor DeVaux, says I. Why, I'll go out and say hello to him. And so I did and so here you are."

"Indeed. Here I am."

The undergraduate squinted up at the sky. "Dark," he said at last, pulling at his ear. "New moon." A thought seemed to occur to him. "I say, it would be a grand night for star watching!"

Jordan reminded himself that laughter would not be considered appropriate in a professor. "I thought I might even go as far as to teach tonight."

Fuller's mouth dropped open. "Lecture tonight?"

"I seem to recall we have a lecture every Wednesday night this term."

The boy looked at him with grave suspicion. *"Every* Wednesday?"

Jordan settled the sleeves of his gown and forced his smile under control. "Whether you're there or not."

He liked Fuller. He shouldn't, perhaps. The boy was hopelessly uninterested in school. Unacademic was the kindest thing one could say. A poll man. Jordan had been Fuller's tutor for three years running, and though the boy's lack of ambition infuriated him, Fuller was too amiable and generous to be anything but likable. Like Arthur in that respect.

Rather than turn back to the tavern, the boy trotted obediently along the road after him. After a few moments walking, he seemed to recall his purpose. "I'm glad I saw you. There was something I wanted to ask."

It was perhaps for the best that his student had interrupted his thoughts, Jordan mused. Phoebe's presence in Cambridge seemed to have locked his mind in a vice grip. "What is it?"

Fuller, who had begun whistling tunelessly, looked stricken. "Can't recall," he said at last with a lop-sided grin.

DeVaux shrugged, and they continued on. It was a lovely night. Warm enough to walk without a great-coat, and if one knew the road as well as he did, pleasant to walk in the dark. There was a serenity that came with the featureless landscape. He'd hoped it would ease his mind, the smooth blackness of the earth and the gaudy spangles of the sky. But tonight the heavens had not worked their usual soothing charm.

It had been madness to bring Phoebe DeVaux here. Why could he not leave well enough alone? It had infuriated her, inconvenienced Hillary, and dis-ordered his own mind to a disturbing degree. In the darkest recesses of his mind, he had the most irri-tating suspicion that he had only done it because he wished to see her.

No, best to put her from his mind. He tried to recall what Fuller had been talking about. He thought back to their last lesson together. "We were discussing the essential features of the Kant and Laplace model of nebula formation."

Fuller looked appalled. "Were we? I must tell you, sir, I had no idea astronomy would be so dashed complicated. Thought it was all about stars. How hard could that be, I said to myself. Better than studying Greek or doing calculus. And now"—he looked vaguely insulted—"I find that to study as-tronomy you need to know both Greek *and* Calculus. Very distressing to be sure."

Fuller walked along, shaking his head. Then a gaping yawn gripped him, paralyzing the length of his whole gangly body. In the middle of it, something in the sky seemed to catch his attention. "See?" he said, finishing up the yawn. "You've ruined the stars for me. I used to look up and think, stars. Now I think, Pollux? Castor? Gemini? Cancer? It's enough to make a decent chap barmy."

"My most abject apologies."

A bony elbow struck Jordan painfully in the ribs. "Remembered!" Fuller exclaimed. "It was about the woman."

"What woman?"

"The woman who came into the dining hall. The beautiful woman."

Jordan made a noise to convey both agreement and annoyance. "She is my cousin's wife." He'd said the phrase a thousand times to himself get used to the idea, to make himself accept it. But even now, nine years later, it sounded strange.

Why was it that even now when she looked at him with those green, green eyes he found himself just as dumbstruck as he had been the first time he'd met her? Did the brain retain nothing it had learned from experience?

Fuller looked crestfallen. "Wife? Too bad. She's bang up to the mark. Haven't seen a creature so easy on the eyes in years. A real lady. Not a girl, like most of the chits around here. A real lady." He cast his eyes up to the stars and sighed. "Your cousin is a very lucky man."

"Not really. He's dead."

In the dark he could not see Fuller's expression, but he suspected it was one of openmouthed astonishment. "A widow?" Fuller said, with something between sympathy and avarice. "Is that so?" He pulled a snuffbox out of his pocket and made a great to-do about inhaling its contents. The man-of-the-world expression Fuller was trying to effect was explosively removed from his face in a fit of sneezing.

So his student admired Phoebe. It was hardly surprising. Jordan felt an unexpected twist of possessiveness, but he ignored it. She was his financial responsibility, that was all. "You're welcome to try your hand at winning her," he said, lengthening his stride. "Though I should warn you, she's as fickle as a woman can be."

He could see the lights of Grantchester in the distance. It was irksome. He'd wanted it completely dark. How could one enjoy a moonless night when there were lights from the towns everywhere? He wished he'd chosen to walk out of town a different way. And then he could have avoided this interview with Fuller altogether. He could have enjoyed the silent clockworkings of the sky in peace.

"Generally," Fuller said gently, "when women discover that I'm heir to the Earl of Warwickshire, they stop being quite so fickle. In fact, I tend to rather break their hearts. On account of their discovering I'm not the marrying kind." He started to take another pinch of snuff, then apparently thought better of it. "But perhaps I should consider becoming the marrying kind. After all, I'm nearly twenty. Will hit my majority soon. Must think about heirs and all that."

Jordan didn't want to discuss Phoebe DeVaux with his student. She was too much in his thoughts already. "The Kant-Laplace model," he said. "Do you recall it?"

"Can't." Fuller replied, then laughed suddenly. "I

can't Kant! That's dashed funny. Should make up some doggerel of some kind. I can't recall Kant. It's lost some Laplace in my head. Ha ha ha! I shall have to write it down when we get home. So the woman, what is her name?"

"Lady Phoebe DeVaux." It was worth what it had been costing him to pay her bills in London just to keep her away from him. What had possessed him to want to stir up those ugly memories? He'd gotten over her long ago.

"Lady Phoebe DeVaux," Fuller repeated, sing-song. "And why was she so angry? She looked quite like Mrs. Siddons. I thought any moment she would brandish a knife and go all wild-eyed."

Phoebe had indeed looked wild. She was going to be more trouble than she was worth, he could tell. "Lady DeVaux can no longer afford to live in London, so she has come to live with my sister and her husband here in Cambridge."

He wondered how much the world knew. Did anyone recall that his name had once been linked with Phoebe's? It wasn't so very long ago. And once they recalled that, there was all manner of gossip they could stir up.

He shouldn't have brought her here. But no, he'd been greedy to see her again—curious, obsessed, name it what you will. And he hadn't been able to resist reasoning that it would be best for her.

Fuller tried to brush a bit of snuff from his sleeve but succeeded only in grinding it into the fabric. "She's very young to be a widow. Was her husband old? Or sickly?"

Jordan kicked a rock and watched it spin off into the darkness. "My cousin was a man of many interests. Unfortunately, a man of many weaknesses as well. He had a great number of friends, but some were unsavory and took advantage of him. Some were jealous of him." He himself had been jealous of his cousin. He paused, recalling Arthur's bonhomie, his charming dissolution. "He was killed in a duel. Lady DeVaux was devastated."

He recalled her tight, white face at the funeral, her eyes blank with a helpless kind of confusion. And here he was, only a year later, dragging her away from her home, likely with some vague, latent hope that he could rekindle their own childish romance. It was sickening.

Fuller smothered another yawn and tried to look properly sympathetic.

"She loved him," Jordan repeated, reminding himself.

His student looked nonplussed. "Thought you said she was fickle. I'd rather a girl be fickle than heartbroken. Can't do a thing about heartbroken."

Jordan made a rather ungracious noise of assent. He looked up at the sky and tried to focus on other things. The stars. Yes, they were all there. The March sky was just as it should be, the planets all in their places. Everything ordered and mathematically correct. He felt his pulse slow. Everything, in the heavens at least, was predictable.

"Perhaps she would like someone to show her about the town," Fuller suggested, the gears of his mind working almost audibly.

"Perhaps." He tried not to picture it. Was Phoebe really so mercenary that she would marry a mere boy like Fuller just for his title? Why not, a bitter voice inside him replied. She'd married for a title before.

It didn't matter. He wasn't her keeper. She could do anything she liked so long as it didn't cost a mint or shame the family name.

He himself needn't see her at all. He had his duties at the university, and he didn't need to go to Hillary's house quite so often as he used to. After all, it would give him more time to write the treatise on meteors he'd been meaning to write.

"She's a diamond of the first water, all right," Fuller mused. "Even if she is a bit mad. She looked quite fierce. Perhaps if one took care not to upset her and kept her away from sharp objects. . . ."

Yes, Phoebe's presence in Cambridge would be a perfect time to prove to himself once and for all that he was over her. Her proximity would explode that vision of her he'd built up in his mind, and she would become ordinary. Just a woman he'd once fancied himself in love with.

Jordan turned around on his heel, suddenly decisive. "It's time for us to go back into town. We're expected at the observatory at eleven."

Four

Hillary was cooing and bouncing the baby on her knee when Phoebe entered the breakfast room. She smiled at Jordan's sister, pressed a kiss to her baby's plump cheek, then went to take a cup from the sideboard.

In the three weeks since she'd been in Cambridge, she'd gotten used to the routines of small-town life, the limited group of acquaintances, the simple pleasures. She'd grown fond of Mrs. Hartfield's cheerful rattlings, her cozy little house, and perhaps even her taciturn husband.

She could not speak as to her feelings about Mrs. Hartfield's brother, since she had not seen the man since she had arrived. Apparently, after winning the struggle over ousting her from the London town house, Jordan had lost interest in her entirely.

She didn't mind. In fact, she preferred it that way. Her life here was not exciting, but it was serene. It was comfortable. Lonely perhaps. Though that was peculiar, considering she now shared a house with far more people than she had in the London house. But any slight loneliness was really inconsequential, as she would not be here long.

Hillary, who despite seeming quite feather-witted

at times, had a sharp head for numbers and was teaching her to keep accounts. Phoebe took great pride in her weekly session, where she offered up for examination the neat columns of income from her annuity and the small properties she held as part of her dowry.

If she was careful, and extremely frugal, it would be less than a year before she could escape. Oh she'd learned her lesson. She had Jordan to thank for that, perhaps. She'd live within her means now. There would never be a need for family to offer her charity again. London of course would not be cheap, but she followed Hillary everywhere, noting her housewifely habits and economizing tricks.

This morning, the windows were open and the breeze and the sunlight played games with the lace curtains. The baby sat on Hillary's lap trying to catch the pattern of cobwebbed shadows that slid across the tablecloth. The creature must have inherited something of his uncle's grave, forbidding manner, for his little forehead was furrowed as he expressed his loud discontentment that the sunlight always managed to evade his chubby grasp.

Hillary laughed at him and kissed his palm. "Good morning, Phoebe," she said cheerfully. "My lamb's got the crotchets today. I can cheer him up, but as soon as I leave off he starts crying again."

"I'm sorry to hear it." Phoebe peered into the wrinkled red face of the infant and smiled. "Are you ill?" she asked, unsure how one was expected to converse with a baby.

She'd known many women with children in London. However, they were of the definite opinion that the presence of a child made their mothers look dowdy, so the offspring were exhibited briefly if necessary, then swept off to the care of nursemaids, tweenys, and governesses.

"You're a cross little bunny, aren't you, my darling?" Hillary put the baby over her shoulder and rose. "You were very good to make him those little shirts, Phoebe. Mine are not nearly so fine, and you know I am always worried about him catching a cold."

"I feel sure he won't. You take such good care of him." Phoebe took a piece of toast and buttered it. When she thought about it, which of course she didn't, it was really rather rude of Jordan to simply drop her in his sister's lap and then never inquire as to how she got on. He likely thought he had done his duty entirely and could now wash his hands of her. Behind the youthful pranks and high spirits of a young man about town, he'd always been such a proper man. Such high, proud notions of honor and duty. And now, now that his days of wildness were behind him, he'd settled quite admirably into the role of the professor: dry, severe, temperate, and inhuman.

"Where is Hartfield?" she said at last, realizing she'd fallen silent for too long.

Hillary looked up from her task of coaxing tiny bits of mashed plum into her child's mouth. Young Master Hartfield, still resentful over the sunlight incident, was having none of this solicitude. "Gone to Grantchester," she replied over the child's wails. "I believe he has gone fishing with Martin Hayhurst and Jeremy Foxborough. They go fishing nearly every fine day in the spring. Doesn't he, my little tulip? Papa will bring home a nice fish for baby's supper." She looked up, her eternally cheerful face beaming. "What shall we do today?"

There seemed to be little choice. In the three weeks since she'd come to Cambridge, Phoebe had discovered that Mrs. Hartfield's entire world consisted of walks in the shrubbery, visits to Mrs. Lane and Lady Hollyfield, and, once a week, a ceremonial trip to Trinity Street to look at the wares in the windows and discuss with great gravity what one would buy if one had the money. No matter how compelling the discussion, they always came home empty-handed.

Phoebe didn't mind, though. The constant, soothing rhythm of their lives was a balm to the unexpectedly disturbing memories that had been stirred up since her move to Cambridge.

"You miss Mama when she goes out, don't you, lovey?" Hillary cooed. "Do you know? I believe he will be cutting a tooth soon. A tooth!"

"Oh." After a moment of silence, Phoebe felt obliged to get up and inspect the child's mouth. "Yes, I believe you are right." Something else was evidently expected so she smiled at them. "Congratulations."

She found that Jordan's sister was looking at her with a peculiar, sad expression that seemed curiously out of place on her good-natured face. "Didn't you and Arthur wish to have children?"

Phoebe removed her finger from the baby's mouth and dried it on a napkin. "Certainly," she said at last. "Unfortunately, we were not blessed with them." She went back to her seat and forced down a bite of bread. It crumbled in her mouth, dry, unswallowable.

She would never admit that Arthur had not touched her in recent years. Even in the beginning, he'd lost interest in her quickly. Just like Jordan, once he'd accomplished what he'd set out to do, he'd quickly embarked on some new crusade.

Hillary flew to her side. "Oh my dear, how careless of me! I should not have said such a thing. I will never forgive myself. Of course you wanted children and now he is gone." Her face crumpled. "And you haven't even a memento of his love." She kissed her own child passionately, and both she and the baby began to cry.

"Nonsense," Phoebe said, patting them both on the head. She'd never felt particularly sorry for herself for being childless. There was certainly no need for anyone else to.

She sat back in her chair. What would it have been like if she had had a child? She found the notion hard to contemplate. She had lived her life so separate from Arthur that it was hard to imagine them having a baby together. Though it might have been nice to have a person in her life who needed her, wanted her.

"I know what will cheer Auntie Phoebe up!" Hillary said, brightening up instantly. "A nice visit to Mrs. Lane. She always makes lemon biscuits on Tuesdays. And we know how Cousin Phoebe loves Mrs. Lane's lemon biscuits."

Phoebe was unsure how she had gained this reputation, as she had merely politely eaten one of the inevitably rock-hard creations each Tuesday. "Would you mind very much if I did not go today?" she asked, carefully. "I have a bit of the headache, and

I would like nothing so much as to sit quietly and finish the book I am reading."

Hillary, surprised, stopped tickling her child under the chin. "Not go to Mrs. Lane's? She'll be very disappointed not to see you. Why, just last week she said that she was looking forward to giving you that recipe for pickling. She'll be terribly cast down when you do not come." Hillary lowered her voice, "She is very set in her habits."

It could be worse. In London Phoebe would have had nothing to talk about but fashion and gossip. At least pickling was a change.

"I know!" Hillary's eyes brightened suddenly. "My little angel will keep you company. I cannot take him with me of course, since it is far too brisk today, and it would be so much nicer if you were to mind him rather than Nanny taking him back upstairs." She looked at Phoebe, her dark eyes so very like her brother's. "Would you?"

The child looked at her, a tiny, malevolent gleam in his eye. Phoebe smiled weakly. "Of course."

As soon as the door closed, the creature began screaming. And screaming. Apparently this miraculous angel had no need to even draw breath, but could produce a continuous stream of noise calculated to reverberate on the eardrum at the most painful frequency. And apparently everyone else in the house was deaf, since no one came into the little morning room to rescue her. "Come on, my dear," she pleaded. "Upsa daisy! Happy baby!" She bounced gently up and down with the child over her shoulder. "No more crying. Happy baby." She peered into his crumpled red face, hoping he wasn't suffocating. At last he stopped crying, took a deep breath, and then began again.

She cooed, she tickled, she threatened, she cajoled. Nothing stopped the continuous wail. "Come on, just for Cousin Phoebe. Be a good little baby."

"Are you torturing my nephew?"

She looked up, relief and annoyance warring within her. "Jordan!" He was the last person she expected to see. And why had he come now, of all times? She felt a self-conscious blush heat her cheeks. He already thought her shallow, fickle, and a spendthrift. Now he would think her blatantly inept with children as well. But why should she care what he thought? She would be free of him soon. Independent. And then she need never see him again.

She pushed a damp curl from her forehead and told her heart to stop its ridiculous antics.

He wore his academic robes, and they still looked strange to her. There was something intriguing about their formlessness. It made one wonder what was underneath.

"Forgive me, I didn't mean to surprise you." His initial smile faded, and he drew himself up with that strange new stiffness he had acquired in the years since they had known each other in London.

She could not help but laugh at the ludicrousness of it all. "Oh, Jordan, what am I to do with this thing? It won't stop."

He came to her and took the baby. She felt heat flood through her as his fingers grazed her bodice, but he didn't seem to notice. For a moment, they were standing very close, with only the small body of the child between them.

"There we are," he said, putting the length of the

room between them. The infant looked quite tiny on his shoulder. He continued to wail, but Jordan gently patted his back, and under the soothing, rhythmic caress, the creature began to quiet.

"How did you do that?" she demanded, ruefully.

He grinned. For a moment he looked like the young man she had known in London. The strange, painful lump in her throat made her wish that he would frown at her as he had before. "I can't very well tell you my secrets. I would lose all credibility with my sister."

She could not help but smile back, though. And she had a feeling she was doing so in the most idiotic way. She walked around behind Jordan's back to look at the child. The baby stared back at her, quite placid now, drooling onto his uncle's shoulder.

She indulged in a brief fantasy that this was her own child and that the broad back before her belonged to her doting husband. It wasn't Arthur she imagined though.

"Where is she?"

"What?" She looked owlishly up at him.

"Hillary?"

"Oh." She came back to her senses. "She has gone to visit Mrs. Lane."

Jordan walked about the room, carefully rocking the little charge on his shoulder. "I should have known. She always visits Mrs. Lane on Tuesdays."

"Always."

"Those dreadful lemon biscuits," he mused. "Someone should tell that woman."

"I'm sorry you missed her. Hillary I mean," Phoebe said, perching on the window seat. Her knees felt suddenly wobbly. Was she actually nervous? How comical. Not a month out of London, and she was acting like a green country girl. "I will tell her you called," she said. She lifted her chin to draw herself together and smiled her most matronly smile. "She'll be terribly disappointed of course. She was saying just this morning that it had been ages since she'd seen you last. You used to come over every Sunday for dinner and every Wednesday night for whist."

"I did," he admitted, a strange expression crossing his face before he turned to make another circuit of the room. The baby had now taken to gumming his collar.

"But you don't anymore." She forced a laugh. "I must say that to break with the established schedule is deemed a serious crime in this household."

He made a wry face but said nothing for a long moment. "I have been busy," he said at last.

Busy? Or avoiding her. She didn't know if she was flattered or irritated. "Did you not come here because I am here?" Heaven knew it didn't matter; after all, he was the one who had deposited her in his sister's household. It was his own fault if he was inconvenienced.

He stopped and pretended to examine one of Hillary's exuberant watercolors on the opposite wall. Over his back she could see the child's eyes were drooping. On Jordan's shoulder he seemed to feel perfectly safe and content. She remembered, vaguely, long ago, laying her own head on his shoulder and feeling the same.

"You didn't wish to see me any more than I wished to see you," he said to the wall.

Phoebe didn't know what she wanted. She realized now that she had longed to see him. She'd hoped he would come to the house. But at the same time, he infuriated her as he always did with his high-handed ways and his coldly aloof reserve. The attraction and repulsion between them would always be there. It was a part of their nature; they were dangerous chemicals that shouldn't be mixed.

That's why they hadn't married, she reminded herself.

"I know you are angry that I brought you here," he continued after a silence. "I know you would have preferred to stay in London. I had hoped that by staying away, I would make life here more comfortable for you."

Comfortable? How could she explain how she felt? It was not comfortable.

When Jordan was in front of her, she could recall, with breathtaking clarity, what it had been like to be held by him, kissed by him. She clenched her teeth and swallowed those impure thoughts.

"The child is asleep," she said, turning the subject. "You have worked a magic charm on him."

He craned his neck back and looked at the baby in his arms. "So he is. Bored, I would imagine. Well, ring for his nursemaid, and we will hope he sleeps until Hillary comes home."

Phoebe complied, wondering if he would leave or if they would be forced to continue the conversation without the youngest Hartfield as a prop. Strangely, she found she didn't want Jordan to leave. She had missed him. In a very normal and platonic way, of course.

She found to her embarrassment that she had

been staring at him. He looked back at her, his expression inscrutable.

"Would you like to go for a walk with me?" he asked, with an expression that said plainly that he wasn't certain himself if it was a wise idea.

"If you like," she said, carefully neutral. Had he spent the last two weeks thinking about her as she'd thought about him? Or was he merely going to reprimand her about some new folly?

Most likely the latter. Jordan didn't appear to be the kind of man who indulged in fantasies of any sort. And he had many more reasons to remember her with bitterness than fondness. She tried to put the past from her mind. "There is something I'd like to talk with you about. And I'd like to see the college. Could you show me the grounds? Is that allowed? Or is it only for students?" She thought for a moment. "Shall I bring a maid? Will people talk if we are seen alone . . . together?"

"You're nattering," he said, and to her surprise, he smiled. "Going all directions at once. You always have."

Some of the tension between them slackened. For the first time, he was admitting that they had been friends once. More than friends, of course, but still friends as well.

"You didn't really think I'd changed, did you?" She smiled back.

He raised his shoulders in the boyish, dismissive gesture she remembered well. "I thought perhaps you'd gotten rather grand in your dotage." Then his voice went soft. "But I'm glad you haven't changed."

Five

Jordan found it unexpectedly pleasant to walk with Phoebe by his side. They fell into step naturally, as though it were the most ordinary thing. He pretended that he was not acutely aware of the small distance between them and the light weight of her hand on his arm. They walked the short distance to Trinity while he pointed out the sites. When they entered the college, he felt anew the pleasure of belonging here. He'd liked London well enough, but this was his home.

"This is the great court," he announced, making an unnecessary gesture toward it. "It was created from Michaelhouse, there, and the King's Hall on that side. The additional structures were added by Thomas Nevile when he was master in the late 1500s." He felt as though he were slipping into lecturer mode so he stifled himself and fell silent.

"And your rooms are there," she said, pointing to the windows on the second floor.

He scowled, remembering that day she had arrived. "Yes."

Had she known then how much her appearance had affected him? How hard it had been not to embrace her? But she was Arthur's widow, and he had refrained, and the moment had safely passed.

He looked around the court, trying to see it as she might see it. It was impressive, graceful even. Hundreds of panes of glass looked down on the court, shining in individual eyes of light.

"There was where Newton had his chambers," he said, pointing. "And there is where Atwood is, and Samuel Vince, the Plumian Chair in Astronomy and Natural Philosophy, is there. Astronomy is one of Trinity's great strengths."

She looked interested, which for some reason gratified him enormously.

"The Bentley observatory was there," he said, pointing to the tower at the top of the gatehouse. "Fine in its day I hear, but dismantled nearly twenty years ago. We use the observatory at St. John's College now. Someday we'll have our own again, I hope. But for the time being we're living on their charity."

He wondered if she'd comment on her own charity status, but instead he felt her tug eagerly at his arm. He allowed her to pull him down the path, deeper into the college court. "How lovely," she said, looking around. "This is more like it. It doesn't seem like a little provincial town at all when you're in here. It's just as grand as anything in London. And such a serious air." She squinted up at him with a thoughtful expression. "I wish ladies could go to school here."

He shrugged his shoulders. "It would be distracting for everyone." Certainly him. He was distracted now, watching the curve of her throat as she looked up at the buildings and the smile that reached her eyes for the first time since he'd seen her in Cambridge.

This was the first day they'd been alone since the day she arrived. The fire inside him made him recall why.

"Would you like to see the library?"

She nodded and he led her through Nevile's Court. The students were walking about and standing in little clusters, but they fell silent and stared when he passed. Professor DeVaux escorting the beautiful woman who'd made that memorable scene in the dining hall. He knew he would be the topic of conversation at dinner tonight. Perhaps there was envy in their expressions as well. Boxty was not the only one who had noticed her beauty. He took her arm possessively and walked a little more quickly.

She did not object, or even seem to notice. Perhaps it seemed natural to her. Though the touch between them was doing strange things to his own physiology.

"Why do they wear robes?" she asked quietly, as though they were strange animals that should not be disturbed. There was something in her confiding whisper that made all his senses ache with longing.

He looked down at her. "Surely you've seen scholars before."

His expression must have been aloof because she scowled. "Of course. I just don't know where the tradition came from. Could they not learn just as well in ordinary clothes?"

"It is to remind them why they are here," he invented, though it sounded fairly correct. "To remind them that they are privileged to be here and that their conduct must be becoming of a scholar. It harks back to the days when all learning was doled out by the church."

She pulled her bonnet closer over her face and ignored a group of men who were goggling her. "I think they look a bit foolish. Like a flock of crows." She looked up at him, suddenly mischievous. "I don't believe I have ever seen you in ordinary clothes."

She had, of course, back in London. But he didn't wish to remind her of it. Their unspoken agreement not to bring up those days should not be breached.

"It would be like seeing a nun out of her habit," he replied. "I would be suddenly transformed into an ordinary being."

She opened her mouth as though she was going to say something, then closed it again.

She was so close to him that the whisper of wind made the fabric of her dress brush against his legs. There was something sensual even in that light contact. He could tell his brain that he'd forgotten her, but his body hadn't. He was a meteor, a fiery mass of futile desires hurtling toward its ultimate destruction. It was madness to have consented to walk with her.

"The library," he said. "Built by Wren, of St. Paul's Cathedral, of course," he heard himself continue, with every appearance of calm. "It's his best work, I think."

She looked up at the long colonnaded structure. It was perfectly symmetrical. Heavy on the bottom, with stately colonnades. Above it was a tier of large glass arches in the gallery. "What is it like on the inside?" she asked, her voice almost reverent.

"I shouldn't show it to you now. There are too

many students there." He smiled. "I'm afraid that the presence of a beautiful woman would distract them."

It was the kind of thing he might have said to any lady, and it would have been taken as merely idle gallantry. But somehow to her it came out sounding strange. He saw her cheeks pinken slightly, but she said nothing.

He guided her out of Nevile's Court and on toward the river that ran close along the back of the library. "What was it you wished to talk about?" he asked, hoping to move more into the role of old friend and advisor. Yes, that was it, old friends. Friends with the bond of their past, but the wisdom to know that their futures lay in different directions.

She looked startled, as though she'd been in the midst of her own reverie. Then she collected herself. "I was thinking," she began at last, "that you might have an idea of what I could *do*."

"Do?" he echoed, when it became clear that she had finished her sentence. "About what?"

Her gaze dropped to the grass, and for a moment she looked almost shy. "About the debt. About those dreadful millinery bills."

He looked at her bonnet, which was all he could see of her averted face. "I had no thought of making you pay them back," he said.

The morning dew on the grassy slope by the river had dried and the backs now looked sunny and inviting. Often in the summer, students flung themselves on the grass to study or merely to pretend to study while they watched the ducks and punts slide along the placid River Cam. It wasn't quite warm enough for that luxury today though, so they turned to walk up the path by the river.

"I want to pay them back." She drew herself up, and looked at him at last, her eyes blazing green. "There is no reason for you to support me. I want to make my own decisions. I want to take care of myself."

He stared at her for a moment. Had she always been so beautiful? What the hell had he been thinking when he let Arthur win her away? He recollected himself and dragged his eyes back to the river. "You are family," he said finally, as though this explained it all. Arthur's wife, not his. But family nonetheless.

He wasn't looking, but he knew she was ruffling up. "I am a burden," she said irritably. "I'm a burden on the family."

She made a move to remove her hand from his arm, but he captured it.

She gave herself a little shake, and he could see the pride raising her chin. "I had no idea I was so in debt. It was naïve of me to have expected Arthur to take care of everything, when God knows, he had little enough idea of economy. But it has happened, and I want to right the situation. Now don't look so shocked, Jordan." She smiled slightly, allowing him to retain her hand. "I am not suggesting I find employment as a companion or a governess." She laughed, though there was still a flush of shame on her cheeks. "Heaven knows I know little enough about children."

He was hurt that she would not accept his settling the debts as a simple favor. As long as she wasn't running up new debts, he was happy. What was this foolish idea of paying him back? He would do no less for any member of his family. He would do more for her. But he had not really reckoned on her pride. "Then what is it that you propose to do?" he asked at last.

She stared across the river for a moment, absorbed in thought. The bells in St. Catherine's faintly began telling the hour, followed more closely by those of King's College Chapel and those of Trinity's own chapel.

"I don't know."

He stopped her, turning her by the shoulders so that she was looking at him. "Forget the idea." He drew a breath. "I know you and I have not been . . . close. But you were Arthur's wife. I would not think of asking you to pay back your bills any more than I would think to ask Hillary the same thing."

He saw her jaw tighten. "I don't want to be in debt to you," she said tightly. "If I pay you back and save up enough besides, I will be able to go back to London."

An unexpected physical pain shot through his chest. "Are you so unhappy with us?" His hands were still on her shoulders, and he was looking her full in the face. Dear God but she was lovely. In another time, a younger, more reckless time, he would have kissed her.

Even now, if he didn't know her, he would have been tempted. Her mouth was so full, her expressive eyes so intently fixed on his own. He recalled with vivid clarity what it had been like to kiss her. She had been eager, giving. She had seemed so sweetly trusting then.

It had been at the opera, in the spring. March perhaps. Still a bit cold and the leaves still tight knots on the trees. They'd been standing at the back of a box, momentarily alone. He had made her laugh about something and then, in a moment of boldness, he had kissed her. He forced the memory back into the dark corner of his mind where it belonged.

"No . . . that is, yes," she was saying. "Yes, I am unhappy. I have nothing to do. No way to make myself useful. I know you're thinking that I wasn't doing anything useful in London, and you're right. I hated that life. But now"—she looked up at him, her expression pleading—"now I want to change that. I don't want to visit Mrs. Lane every Tuesday. I don't want to have a life that is nothing but whist and babies. It is all right for some people, Jordan. I'm not criticizing your sister. But it isn't all right for me."

"You can't go back to London." The words were out, sounding harsher than he'd meant for them to. He told himself it was because he didn't trust her not to return to her profligate ways in Town, but he knew it wasn't true. There was something else there that he didn't really want to examine.

She shrugged off his hands and turned away from him, angry. "You brought me to this godforsaken place where I am nothing but a poor relation. If you mean to teach me a lesson, you have done so. But I never thought you were the kind of man who would stoop to that after so many years."

"It is not a punishment," he protested, following her as she walked down to the river. "I . . . that is *we* felt it best that you stay here. Hillary wanted you here. She felt you would be lonely all on your own in London."

"Lonely?" she spat back at him. "I was not lonely there. I am lonely here."

Whom did she miss? Arthur? Yes, that was all right; Arthur had won her fair and square. Besides, she could miss a dead man here just as easily as in London. His loss wasn't making her lonely here. Whom was she missing? A stranger?

He felt a sudden surge of anger. "Did you leave a lover in London, Phoebe?" His stomach twisted at the thought. "I shouldn't be surprised. It is the done thing in Town, I believe."

Her lack of response only infuriated him further. "Perhaps he could send you money to get you out of here. Buy you back from me, if you will," he said cruelly. "Or is he poor? That would be rather endearing. Perhaps once you had your titled husband, you decided to take a lover for whom you actually had a real fondness."

He was saying too much but he couldn't seem to stop the sudden rush of long-dammed bitterness.

Her face was the cold, inexpressive mask he had seen the night she had first arrived. "There was only one man I loved in London," she said in a tight, cold voice. "And you know very well that it was . . . was . . ." She looked quite stricken for a moment, then defiant. ". . . that it was Arthur."

Six

Phoebe stalked home from the market, her head down and her arms crossed across her chest. How provoking it was to live in a small town. The man at the cheese shop had been personally affronted when she asked if he carried anything French; the baker had tried to cheat her out of sixpence; and the chandler had had the cheek to ask how she enjoyed her walk on the backs with Professor DeVaux yesterday.

It had been humiliating enough to quarrel with him like a fishwife, but the idea that the entire town was snickering over it was too much. Hadn't they better things to do than watch an irritable exchange between two people who couldn't seem to go more than a few minutes in each other's company without exchanging words?

As she turned up the walk to the house, there was a strange rustling in the hedges and a tall, lanky man jumped out.

She gave a cry of alarm, then stifled herself as she realized that the young man was a student, and that he was far more startled by her response than she had been at his sudden appearance.

"I'm sorry, I didn't mean to frighten you," he

said, looking balefully at the bush from which he'd emerged. "I was just . . . er . . . I was just waiting for you."

"In the bushes?"

He blushed up to the brim of his hat. "Wanted to be sure I caught you."

She could not help but smile back at him. "Why?"

He looked as though this were the best question she could possibly have asked. "Luncheon. That is, I've brought a picnic luncheon, and I thought you might want to come along on a punting luncheon party. I was at the house, but there's no one at home. It isn't proper to introduce myself, I know, but I did so want to invite you along."

At her blank look he seemed to recall himself. "I'm Stanhope Fuller, that is, Viscount Stanhope Fuller." He swept off his hat. "I'm just Boxty Fuller to most everyone. Lord knows why. Just one of those names that sticks, I suppose. I'm at Trinity College. You might have seen me the other night. The night you arrived."

She hadn't, of course. In their caps and gowns all the students had appeared entirely interchangeable. "Lord Fuller," she said, shaking the hand he offered. "I'm Lady Phoebe DeVaux."

"Lady DeVaux, yes I know. That is, that's what Professor DeVaux said. But you're not related to him, are you?"

"Only by marriage," she ground out, her annoyance returning.

"Yes, well. I thought that was the case. You'd think, with the same last name that you might be, but you're not."

"No."

He stared at her with an expression of perfect contentment.

"Would you like to come in for some tea?" she offered at last, not seeing another way to be rid of him.

"No, that is, I was hoping we could have the luncheon. Unless of course you'd prefer tea. I have tea. In a flask. But perhaps you'd prefer your own tea."

His rattling unaccountably made her smile. "I couldn't very well lunch with you on my own, you know," she said, hoping to dissuade him. "Though it was very kind of you to ask me."

The last thing she needed was to get a reputation in Cambridge for indiscretion. Jordan's insulting accusation still burned hotly within her.

"Oh!" he said, looking quite pleased. "There's a whole party of us going. And," he added, as though playing his trump card, "I asked Professor DeVaux to accompany us."

"Jordan?" Absolutely not. After yesterday's insulting exchange, she had little desire to ever see the man again.

Her swain was absorbed in trying to extract a large basket from the hedge. He looked up. "Jordan? Oh, Professor DeVaux. I suppose that is his Christian name. I suppose it couldn't have been 'Professor.' Though that would have been dashed funny if it were." He laughed his donkey bray laugh. "Wish my parents had thought to name me something clever. 'Your Highness' might have been good. Then everyone would have to walk about saying 'Yes, Your Highness,' 'No Your Highness' to me." He laughed again, then sobered. "Though I suppose the King might have had something to say about that."

He tapped his chin for a moment in thought, caught sight of the basket in his hands, and recalled what he had been saying. "Yes, Professor DeVaux said he'd go with us. So you see, it's all right and tight."

"He said he'd go with us?" she echoed, stupidly.

"Certainly. Said he'd meet us by the launch. There's a whole group of us going. We'll punt down toward Harston and then have a luncheon." He looked taken aback by her suspicious expression. "Now you think I'm bamming you. You think I'm going to lure you off with false promises of an escort." For a moment he looked rather wounded at being thought capable of such villainy.

"Professor DeVaux said you wouldn't go," he continued. "He said I could invite you but that you wouldn't." His pale blue eyes were wide and hopeful. "I said you would. After all, I went all the way to Great Shelford for the pasties. And it is such a lovely day to go out. Have you gone punting?"

"No," she admitted. Though the prospect was intriguing. Only not with Jordan.

"I shall take you. It's everything proper. Particularly with the professor there. You know what a stickler he is."

"Yes." Jordan was everything cold and correct.

"And Professor Caldwell will be there too. So it's doubly correct. Will you go?"

Lord Fuller looked so eager, and so alarmingly young. Her first instinct was to turn him off politely, just in case he'd get the wrong impression. But he didn't look lovestruck, only like a happy puppy anxious for attention.

Jordan might have forced her to come to Cambridge, but she was capable of living her life however she liked. She had vowed when Arthur died that she would no longer be constrained by society's dictates.

"I'll get my spencer," she said, turning up the walk toward the house.

She ran upstairs, bemused to find herself looking forward to the picnic far more than she'd expected to. After all, it was the first outing she'd had since she arrived. Little wonder she was starved for amusement.

As it was Saturday, Hillary and her husband had driven over to Hartfield's mother's house as they always did, so she left a message with the butler and went to join Lord Fuller.

As promised, Jordan was waiting at the launch. They caught each other's eye quite by accident as she was coming up the path, but he assiduously avoided her gaze until they had come within speaking distance.

"I told you I'd convince her," Fuller said gleefully. "She's never been punting before. Isn't that a laugh? We'll have such a grand time." He made a gesture toward Jordan as though he were introducing them. "Professor DeVaux is my Trinity tutor you see. So he's obliged to help me with all the other subjects I'm studying in besides his own."

Lord Fuller seemed oblivious to the tension between her and Jordan. Determined to keep the peace, Phoebe gave Jordan what she hoped was a cordial nod.

"Now, I know I'm not the most needle-witted of

fellows," Fuller went on. "I'd have been sent down long ago if it hadn't been for the professor here. Don't believe I'll ever graduate," he admitted, ruefully.

"Of course you will," Jordan said firmly. "It's merely a matter of applying yourself." He turned and gave Phoebe a faint smile. "Come, Lady DeVaux, I'll hand you in. One can not live a full month in Cambridge and avoid punting the Cam."

She looked at his face as he helped her into the boat. He seemed to have entirely forgotten their quarrel. He appeared relaxed, pleasant, entirely at ease. Why could she not feel as serene? She was still riled at their exchange, but he was as calm as the night sky.

He looked past her and smiled. "Ah, here is Caldwell."

Fuller looked up and waved at the group of people approaching. "Here's Grinny and Joxer and Mad Jack. I see Jack's brought his sister. I wish he hadn't. She's always throwing herself at my head. Grinny's mad about her, but of course, just to be perverse, she won't have anything to do with him. And Professor Caldwell's brought his violin so we shall have music. What a jolly party."

Everyone was introduced, helped into punts, and given hopelessly detailed instructions on finding the picnic site.

"As you can see, the whole world's at it today," Fuller said, squinting at the boats on the river. "We shall be hard-pressed not to ram anyone. But whenever it is a fine day, everyone is out."

Once he had assured himself that she was comfortably settled in the narrow boat, Fuller took the stern and began poling them down the river.

"How lovely," she exclaimed, unable to keep the cool mien she had sworn to maintain. "I've found at last the ideal way to travel." It was a cloudless day, the sky the flat blue that only comes on a perfect day in April. The river was utterly smooth, ruffled only where other boats were moving. As Fuller had said, the whole world was out today, and the river was so full that she could have walked across the river going from boat to boat. But as it was, she was content to sit back and watch the willows at the banks slide by.

"It was good of you to chaperone," she said, slanting Jordan a look. "One never knows the kind of mischief I might have gotten into if you were not here to keep me in check."

He pulled at his cravat and had the grace to look slightly embarrassed. "I'm sorry I said what I did, Phoebe. It was inappropriate of me."

She felt slightly mollified. "Let us forget that meeting," she suggested, hoping he didn't remember it as well as she did. She'd been angry at his accusation, but there had been something else. Something more disturbing. She hoped he hadn't read in her eyes the extremely unchaste thought that she had been thinking. His touch had that unsettling effect on her.

Even now she was experiencing burning flashes of memory. She remembered the night he had kissed her at the opera. Her life had changed forever then. And for a moment, she had truly believed that her future held nothing but joy.

Jordan opened his mouth and drew his breath as though he was going to say something, then stopped, started again, and finally shook his head.

"I thought we'd go down beyond the pool," Fuller said, breaking the tension at last. It's further than most people go, and we'll find a nice spot." He grinned. "The advantage of being obliged to repeat courses as often as I have is that one gets to know all the secrets of the area quite well."

Phoebe braced her arms behind her, leaned back, and closed her eyes. The sun through the trees dappled the light behind her lids and warmed her face. She thought vaguely of removing her spencer, but decided it wasn't worth the bother. It was so very comfortable.

"Has she fallen asleep?" she heard Fuller ask, sounding a little insulted.

"I don't know," Jordan replied. She felt him lean closer. "Are you asleep, Phoebe?"

She knew if she opened her eyes his face would be close to hers. Instead she kept them closed and smiled. "Oh yes. Fast asleep," she assured them.

"Excellent. Then we may talk about her," Boxty said cheerfully. "She's remarkably beautiful."

"She's too old for you, Fuller."

"Not true! I'm a man of the world. Heir to a useless title and lots of dull properties. I've plenty to offer a woman."

"I hear she has a terrible temper," Phoebe offered, her eyes still closed.

"And a flair for drama," Jordan added.

"I believe I saw that when she walked into the dining room." Fuller laughed.

"Utterly incorrigible," she agreed cheerfully. "You'd far better give up and let her go back to London than try to reform her here."

"She'll stay here."

Phoebe opened her eyes a little to see if Jordan was quizzing her, but he looked rather serious. She frowned. They still had that battle to fight.

Lord Fuller sighed and continued to pole the boat down the river. "Will she ever marry again, do you think?" he said at last.

She sat up straighter, all sleepiness gone. "No. I don't believe she will." The game was too personal now, and Jordan was sitting too still and too silent. "We seem to have left most of the crowds behind," she said, looking about her and hoping to change the subject. "Are we nearly at the spot you picked?"

"Do you see that tree there? The one with the spreading branches?" Fuller nodded at one some distance ahead at a bend in the river.

"Yes."

"It isn't that one." He laughed a long time. "Have patience. It will be worth it."

"I shouldn't have come," Jordan muttered.

"No," she agreed, "you are in a perfectly dreadful mood. I don't know why you agreed to chaperone."

His placid veneer was back in place. "Someone had to."

"But not you. You are obviously not in the mood for an outing, and you will ruin it for the rest of us with your crossness." She said it lightly, but she meant it too. Boxty Fuller didn't seem to feel inhibited by the presence of his mentor, but she certainly did. The man was breathing down her neck like a carrion crow.

"Now"—she shook her finger playfully in his face—"no more thinking whatever you're thinking. We're having a nice luncheon and that is that. I won't have you—"

"Why did you end our engagement?"

She stared at him for a moment, stunned. "Jordan, I hardly—"

"It's been nine years. Surely now you can tell me why."

She cast a glance at Fuller, but he was calling back to the two other boats, directing them to the landing spot. "I don't think this is the time."

Jordan was looking at her, his dark eyes intense, burning into her. For a moment, beneath that calm facade he'd cultivated, she could see the passionate man she had known so long ago.

"And don't tell me it was because you'd fallen in love with Arthur," he said in a low, tight voice. "It isn't true. You'll tell me that I don't know you, and yes, now that is true. But I knew you then, Phoebe. And I know you didn't love Arthur."

She looked out over the river and schooled her features into something like his own placidity. Her mind was running with all the frantic, futile madness of a rabbit with the hounds at its heels. She had to say something. But was this the time for the truth?

"You did not love me," she said, the words tearing out of her at last. "And at the time, I thought that was necessary in a marriage."

His brows snapped together in an expression of pain she had not anticipated. "Phoebe, how can you say that? You know I—"

"I saw you kiss Lady Whitcombe," she interrupted. She felt as though she were pushing the words out as her throat closed around them. "It was that spring, in London. Shortly after we got engaged. You were putting her into a carriage, and you kissed her. That's when I knew you didn't love me."

Silence.

Instead of guilt, she saw confusion. Then bewilderment. Then realization. Then at last, guilt. "Phoebe—"

"That very day you'd sworn your heart belonged to me, that you were mine forever, all that kind of poetic nonsense. And there you were, kissing someone else."

"Phoebe, I—"

"So you see," she continued with horrible cheer, "I'm afraid it never would have worked. The whole world likely knew of your relations with Lady Whitcombe, and I was the last." She gave him an acid smile. "How stupid you made me feel. I denied it until I saw it with my own eyes."

"Phoebe, I hardly knew Lady Whitcombe. There was nothing—"

She did not want to hear his feeble excuses. She was beyond all that now. He'd made his decisions, and she'd made hers. And she'd thought her decision to marry Arthur had been irrevocable, permanent. But now Arthur was dead and here they were struggling again with the undeniable attraction that had always been between them.

She looked out over the pastoral countryside. "Lord Whitcombe killed my husband, you know. How strange that between the two of them, the Whitcombes have taken from me the two men I cared for most." Her eyes locked with his. "Whitcombe never knew about your liaison with his wife, did he? How ironic. It was you he should have killed on the field of honor."

It was a cruel thing to have said, and she immediately wished the words back in her mouth. But they were said and so she sat there, staring at him, defiant.

"Yes," he said slowly at last. "I expect that would have been more convenient for everyone involved."

Seven

At last they reached the site Boxty had decided upon. It really was lovely, with the surrounding willows dipping their delicate leaves into the water and a grassy slope that ran right down to the water's edge. The party managed to tie their boats to the trees and scramble out without the loss of even one of the picnic baskets, though a loaf of bread was dislodged and went floating downstream as it was savaged by ducks, and Fuller ended up with one wet trouser leg.

"Let me help you."

Phoebe looked up from the place they'd picked on the grass and saw Professor Caldwell coming toward her. She handed him the basket she'd taken charge of, and they began unpacking the luncheon. They conversed on the most banal of topics, but she could not resist shooting him a worried glance. He'd likely been there the night she'd burst in on their dining hall. He must think her a complete hoyden.

"Are you enjoying Cambridge, Lady DeVaux?" he asked. "I'm from London myself, so I can vouch that it takes a while to get used to the slower pace of our town."

"I do like it," she said honestly.

There was a great deal of bantering and shrieking over the unpacking of the second basket. Phoebe had the strong suspicion that the exercise was merely an excuse for Fuller's friend Grinny to show off in front of Mad Jack's sister and for that young lady to put herself very much in the way of Lord Fuller. "It's much livelier than I thought," she added wryly.

"Best put a stop to that," Caldwell said with a grin that she could not help returning. He got to his feet and wandered over to the group of young people. His very presence had a chastening effect, and the group completed their task in a silence broken only by the occasional explosive giggle.

Caldwell gave her a conspiratorial wink. Now, he was handsome enough with his boyish grin and rus- set hair. Why didn't he make her heart leap wildly in her body as though it were trying to escape?

She shot a glance toward Jordan, but he was en- gaged in seeing that Mad Jack's sister was protected from Grinny's relentless advances.

Once they were all settled under the grove of trees near the water, Fuller helped her fill her plate. "Don't know why the professor is in such a huff," he confided to her in a low voice. "He's usually such a laugh."

"Don't mind him," she assured him. "You've made such an effort over lunch that we will do ev- erything to enjoy it. Tell me what it is like being at Trinity. Such lovely grounds."

"Indeed, it's good fun," he said, downing a piece of meat pie in two bites. "Guess I must like it, or I would have given it up long ago. I don't really have the brains for university, you know. But I don't mind too much." He shrugged and took another slice of pie. "We all have lots of larks, the other lads and I. The lectures are interesting, Professor DeVaux explains everything I don't quite get the run of, and then he teaches these grand lectures in the middle of the night."

"Ah, yes, Hillary mentioned them."

She shouldn't have let Jordan bring up the past. After all, what had happened had happened and there was little point regretting it. She'd married Arthur; he'd disappeared into the depths of Cambridge, and that was that.

"They're brill!" Joxer exclaimed. "We go to the St. John's College observatory, and we have a bit of a lecture, and then we get to take turns looking through the telescope."

"How fascinating," she said, interested in spite of herself. "What do stars look like up close?"

Fuller waved a dismissive hand. "About the same. But the planets, now they're interesting."

She sat up straighter, her fork arrested on its way to her mouth. "I don't suppose I ever thought about the planets. You must think me very stupid—" She slanted a look at Jordan, but he was talking quietly to Caldwell, who was engaged in tuning his violin. "—but I don't think I could tell them apart."

"Oh you could through the telescope at the observatory," Joxer assured her. "Planets are grand. Some green, some red, Saturn with its hoops of course. It's dashed bizarre to think of them out there, whirling about just like the earth. Makes you think, I'll tell you that. Makes you feel very small."

"I imagine that it would."

Jordan had leaned back on his arms and was contemplating the leafy crown above them. "But it's all very regulated," he put in, joining the conversation for the first time. "All very predictable."

"And it will keep going on the way it's always gone on for all the forever we can imagine," added Caldwell. He gave the group a roguish smile and started up a tune on the violin. It was an old one, lilting and sweet, with a slight melancholy air beneath the cheerful melody. Somehow it seemed perfectly suited to a picnicking party on the river.

Fuller scratched his nose and looked a bit doubtful. "See the professors like the math parts," he continued in a low voice. I have to admit, if I'd known there was so much arithmetic, I wouldn't have taken astronomy. I thought it would be a great deal more looking at the stars and predicting the future and all that kind of thing."

"You can predict the future," Jordan said, unexpectedly. He sat up and looked at them. "If you do the calculations, you can predict exactly where the stars will be next. And with a bit more work, you can predict the trajectories of the comets, and the timing of eclipses, and when the planets will pass each other in that great polonaise." He waved a hand toward the sky. "And yet, predictable as it is, there is always mystery."

There was a strange look about him. He was flushed and his eyes were bright. She had not seen him this way in a long time. It was almost like the look of a man in love. Did he care so much then for his work in astronomy? Phoebe felt a newfound sense of respect. It was a side of him she had not seen before. A part of him that had developed since they parted.

She felt a pang of what nearly felt like jealousy. He had never been so passionate, or so devoted, to her.

Boxty Fuller made a face. "He gets quite on a high horse about it sometimes," he said confidingly.

Mad Jack's sister, who was obviously fully enjoying the attention she was receiving, insisted that she be allowed to dance, and so Caldwell obligingly played a country air and Phoebe was recruited to make up the set.

She partnered Fuller, then Joxer, and even suffered Mad Jack's uncoordinated exuberance. Jordan, however, did not join them.

She noted, however, that his gaze was often upon her, grave and unsmiling.

"Would you like to take a walk, Lady DeVaux?" asked Fuller, after they'd exhausted even Miss Mad Jack's enthusiasm. He shot a worried glance at the girl, who had shown a tenacious tendency to cling to his arm more than she should. "The pigeon pie was rather heavy. I'm afraid there isn't much choice around here. I'm sure in London there are hundreds of places to get pigeon pie."

Phoebe allowed Fuller to lead her away from the group. She shot a glance at Jordan, but he seemed absorbed in his own thoughts, removed from the dancers and the music. "Don't go too far," he called out after them, just when she thought he'd not noticed her going. "And slap him if he's impudent, Phoebe."

She tried to laugh, but it caught in her throat. She wished more than ever she had not answered his question about why she had ended their engagement. It didn't matter anymore, and it had only hurt them both.

And of course it had been only half-truth. She'd seen the way he'd kissed Eleanor Whitcombe. It was affectionate, but not loverlike. At the time, though— Well, at the time things had been very different.

She began a stately promenade along the banks of the river with Fuller.

"Do you like London, Lord Fuller?" she asked, just to have something to say.

"Please call me Boxty. Everyone else does. I don't know who you're talking to if you Lord Fuller me." He smiled at her in his open, friendly way. "No, I hate London. Too dashed big. A man can't find his bearings there. I have to go occasionally to see my parents, you know. But they're always throwing fancy rig-ups, and I never know anyone or have any fun.

"I have much more of a lark down here. Though mind you, I wouldn't want to live here forever either. When you've been here as long as I have, it seems a bit dull. It would be a better place if one didn't have to study all the time."

She'd spent every minute since she got here wanting to go back to London, but now, as she looked around at the placid river and the university buildings in the distance, she wondered if it wasn't a rather nice place after all.

"I wouldn't mind going on the grand tour," Boxty continued. "That would be everything exciting." His mouth turned down in a comical expression of disappointment. "But I can't go until I graduate. And that will likely be never."

He looked serious for a moment. "I don't know what I will do when I graduate. If I graduate. Either way, they'll throw me out at some point. I so dread having to take my place in the Lords. No fun at all in that."

He looked so sad that she felt a sudden wave of sympathy for him. "You could stay on and teach," she suggested. "Look at Professor DeVaux."

He raised his bony shoulders in an expressive shrug. "Don't have the brainbox for it. A poll man to the last. Ah well. If you like London there must be something to it. And you do like it, don't you? I heard the professor say once that you were bored to flinders in a provincial town like this."

It wasn't so bad now that she had found more interesting things to do than go on visits and take shopping trips. "Yes, I liked London very much. I'm going to go back there, you know."

"When?" He looked horrified.

She laughed. "Not for a long time, I'm afraid. See, I owed quite a bit of money there. Professor DeVaux was very kind to pay off everything, but one can't live comfortably owing someone money like that."

Boxty nodded vigorously, "A debt of honor."

Now that the dancing had stopped, Caldwell was playing a low, sad song that somehow seemed to speak to Phoebe's heart. Was it really melancholy she'd been feeling of late? She tried to recall the last time she had felt truly, truly happy.

It was that night at the opera house. Nine years ago.

"So you'll go back to London?" Boxty prompted. "When you've saved up enough?"

"I haven't much income," she confessed. "Not

very much at all. But what I do have, I'm saving and I'm learning how to manage."

"Sounds ghastly."

"Actually, it's far more interesting than I thought it would be," she said, latching on to the subject with enthusiasm. "I was shockingly profligate before, largely because I never knew anything about managing money. And I never saw the bills, since they went to my husband, and I never thought much about where the money was to come from. Hillary is very good with money. She knows exactly when it is worth buying something less expensive and when it is not. Do you see this lace?" She flourished her cuff in front of him. "I got it for four shillings. In London I would have paid three times as much and never batted an eye."

She could see Boxty's eyes starting to wander. "So I'm saving my money to pay back what I owe DeVaux and then I shall go back to London entirely afloat," she concluded triumphantly. "I'll be independent. A merry widow."

Down the river, Caldwell had finished playing and the group on the grass was talking and laughing. Phoebe felt like she did sometimes with the Hartfields. Like she was on the outside looking in.

"Why London?" asked Boxty. "Could you not be independent somewhere else? I should think London would be a dashed inconvenient place to be independent."

"No, London is the only place for it," she insisted. "There no one cares for you at all. If you want to wear your bonnet backward, people don't pay any mind. Of course, in most select circles, people watch you and censure you just the same as if you were in any horrid gossipy little small town. But when you're merely a slightly impoverished widow of no distinction, no one will think twice about anything you do."

Boxty looked mildly insulted. "I wouldn't say that you are of no distinction."

She shrugged. Boxty couldn't understand. He didn't know how galling it was to have to have Jordan step in and save her. And him of all people.

"I'm terrible with all things financial," Boxty said, pulling up a tall stalk of grass as he walked. It was fluffy at the end, with a little plume like the feathery white flame of a candle. He drew it through his hand and thousands of tiny seeds broke off and drifted away. They lit like snow on the grass. "Profligate, my father says. Hopeless."

"Oh but you're not hopeless!" Phoebe exclaimed. "I thought I was as well. I thought there was no way I could live if I didn't spend exactly what I was spending. But I have found that I quite enjoy knowing where my money goes. I'm not terribly good at it yet. I still don't really understand what goes on on the 'change, but Hartfield is very good about explaining it to me."

"Was your husband in debt then?" Boxty asked.

"Shockingly so. I'm afraid he really was a hopeless case." She walked along for a moment in silence. "Arthur loved to gamble you see. And I got a taste for it myself. I suppose just out of boredom, really. But with Arthur it was as though he could not live without it."

When she gave it much thought, she realized how very lonely her life with Arthur had been. They did nothing together, except perhaps gamble. At the time, she did not think much of it. After all, most of the other married ladies she knew did not expect more from their husbands. She wondered why, now, it should suddenly seem so entirely unsatisfying.

He had spent the evenings at his club. She had gone to the theater and to balls with her friends. Friends she never heard from now. No, life in London next time would be very different.

"Known men like that." Boxty shook his head. "They can't stop no matter how they try. We tied Joxer to the bed at one point to keep him from it, but he chewed through the ropes and went to Newmarket just the same."

She sighed. "Poor Arthur. He didn't mean to be what he was." She felt a shudder pass through her, but suppressed it. "He just wanted to win and that was that. Win at everything. He'd bet a three-legged dog could beat a Welsh pony and still be convinced he'd come out the winner." She felt strange, as though she'd said too much. Too many memories came flooding back. Dark ones. Ones she didn't want to recall. "But he always meant well," she assured Boxty. For some reason she felt rather nauseated.

The man's open face drooped with sympathy. "I'm sorry if I made you upset when I asked if you would marry again. I shouldn't have said that."

Phoebe looked back toward where the group was sitting. To her surprise, Jordan's face was turned toward her. As they walked toward him she could see that he was staring at her with an odd speculative expression, as though he were trying to fathom her very mind. She felt a blush rise up her cheeks.

"Oh please don't feel badly," she assured Boxty with a high laugh that sounded slightly forced. "I hope I wasn't rude to you. I only meant that I don't think I ever will remarry. Once was quite enough." She broadened her smile and took his arm. "Now that I am a respectable widow, I can do anything I like. I shall likely become entirely eccentric. Perhaps I'll take my notions of economy to extremes and begin turning my gowns and forbidding the maids to have candles." She laughed. "The freedom may go entirely to my head."

For the first time though, the notion of freedom sounded a bit lonely.

Eight

Jordan walked down the street to Hillary's house with a certain sense of hesitation. It was twilight, an inconvenient time to be about, with the unpaved road treacherously dark and the infrequent carriage leaping out of the gloom when one least expected it. But he'd resisted going to Hilary's house for nearly a week and a half, and he couldn't wait any longer.

Phoebe's confession as to the reason she'd broken their engagement bewildered him. He couldn't even recall with clarity the incident she'd mentioned. He remembered the day of course. He'd merely been helping Eleanor Whitcombe with her travel arrangements, and she'd been upset, and well, perhaps he *had* kissed her. But his thoughts at the time had not been passionate.

On the one hand it was infuriating that his engagement to Phoebe, their whole future together, had ended because of something so meaningless.

And on the other hand, it meant, perhaps, that there was hope now.

It was a lovely evening. It was the exact point where spring stops being wet and miserable and begins to flirt with the idea of actually becoming something lovely. He smiled up into the sky. It would be a perfect night, dark and clear. Perhaps he'd go to the observatory later and watch the sky revolve. But first, Phoebe. He quickened his step.

The Hartfields' house sat like a fat little lantern on the corner. Annie, the silly girl, had neglected to draw the drapes and the light spilled out from every window. He paused for a moment, watching the little pantomime show within. Upstairs, the nanny sat by her lamp, sewing. Two of the house-maids were huddled over a letter, laughing, and Annie herself was making slow progress closing the drapes of the upstairs drawing room. Though she looked directly at him, he could tell by her blank expression that she could not see him in the dark.

Which room was Phoebe's? The yellow one, most likely. It was the nicest. His eyes found the room of their own volition, but Annie had been there before him and shut off his view. He shouldn't be looking anyway, he reminded himself.

Still, his heart began an erratic dance when he saw the whole family gathered around the card table in the downstairs drawing room. Convincing himself that a moment's pause would calm the arrhythmia, he watched them.

It was all so ordinary, it was fascinating. And even though the Hartfields and Phoebe did nothing but sit looking intently at the cards they held, making occasional comments, sipping miniscule glasses of sherry, it was magical. Phoebe looked more relaxed than she ever did in his presence. True, there were times when a tiny frown formed between her brows, but it was impossible to tell whether it was brought on by her thoughts or merely the cards she held.

When she laughed, however, there was a warmth to her face that he had never seen before. For some reason, it gave him a rather empty feeling below his ribs.

He shook himself, mounted the steps, and in a moment, was admitted into the golden glow of the house.

He waved the maid away and indicated that he would announce himself. He didn't, however, and instead hung in the doorway, still loath to interrupt the cozy scene.

"Oh my," his sister was saying, in a tone of abject misery, "two of clubs. What will I do now?" She chewed her lip. "Oh dear, oh dear. Laurence, do look at my cards and tell me what I should do."

Her husband looked over her shoulder, plucked out a card, and threw it on the table.

"Oh yes, of course. I should have thought of that, to be sure." She sighed. "Oh, Phoebe, it is such a pity there aren't two of you. Then we should be able to play whist. I'm not much better at whist, mind you. In fact, I daresay Hartfield would not play with me even if there were enough of us, because he knows I cannot keep it straight. So perhaps we'd better wish there were three of you so that Hartfield would be excused from playing with me entirely."

Hartfield grunted what sounded like assent, and went back to his cards.

Both women burst out laughing, but their laughter was cut short when they spotted Jordan in the doorway.

"Jordan!" his sister exclaimed, going to him. "Is it really you? I was entirely convinced you'd gone off to the Continent or been thrown in jail, or had an accident. We've seen neither hide nor hair of you for ages."

"Very naughty of me," he admitted. He could not meet Phoebe's eyes. He knew very well that he could not conceal the hungry expression in his own and so it was best that they not exchange glances. "I am here now, though perhaps at an inopportune time. I didn't mean to interrupt your play."

"My wife plays so badly you can hardly call it playing. Phoebe's better, but she's too softhearted. Keeps trying to give over good cards to Hil. Thinks I don't notice." Hartfield gave a snort and gathered up the cards. "Busy of late, making sure the stars are all still there?"

"Something like that." He couldn't very well admit he'd been mooning about like a fool, rereading yellowed letters, staring at a miniature of a golden-haired girl with a warm, open smile. He took the seat his sister offered. "What have you been doing of late, Hillary?"

"Hillary and I have been going through the household accounts," Phoebe volunteered unexpectedly, going to sit on the hearth rug with the baby in order to ensure that he did not succeed in eating the coal or knocking himself over the head with the poker. "We have saved twelve pounds this quarter by going to a different chandler." There was an almost defiant tone to her voice. Jordan looked up to see that she was looking directly at him.

"Phoebe has become quite good at spotting mistakes in tradesmen's bills and discovering new ways to economize," Hillary added. "I daresay Hartfield didn't notice that the butter was any different, but it costs us nearly twopence less a pound."

"Don't give a hang about butter," Hartfield assured them.

"Oh, it isn't that," Hillary replied. "I merely don't like to pay more than I should. Phoebe and I make a little game of it."

Phoebe grabbed the child as he launched himself toward the coal hod. "I never did the household accounts before," she admitted. "Arthur took care of everything. He told me he didn't want me to worry about it."

Jordan saw Hillary's face take on that pinched look it always had when anyone mentioned Arthur. His sister had been as passionate in her dislike of their cousin as he had been fond. Even as a child, she had run from him, spurned his most charming offers of friendship, and had done everything short of cutting him when they were adults. Strange. Arthur and Hillary had been the two people he'd counted as his closest companions. But the two had never managed to get along.

"Perhaps, my dear," Hillary said with admirable tact, "it was because he didn't want you to know where the money went." Her expression changed. "No my love! Don't grab that. It's hot. Very very hot." She swooped the baby into her lap and tried to interest him in a wooden horse that apparently held much less attraction than the lion-headed andirons.

"Yes," Phoebe said at last, "Arthur wasn't good with money at all."

The mention of his name seemed to have put a damper on the conversation. The fire in the grate snapped and the baby banged the wooden horse against the leg of the table.

"How's my nephew?" Jordan asked at last, unable to think of anything better.

"He's got the slightest sniffle," Hillary provided, handing the baby over to him. "But he's been a perfect angel considering the tooth, haven't you been, sweetikins? Show Uncle Jordan the tooth."

The baby's glossy lower lip protruded for a moment, then its mouth opened up like a letterbox, and it began to wail.

"I was thinking," he said, getting to his feet and pacing the length of the room with the child in his arms, "that you all might like to go to the observatory." How stupid. He hadn't had that thought until this very moment.

"At St. John's College?" his sister asked. "It's quite late for an outing, don't you think?" She had apparently given up on his ability to properly admire her progeny's dental prowess and came over to examine the child's tooth herself. "Why, I do believe there is a second one coming in as well! Isn't that something? Two teeth! Little lambkins has two teeth!" She took the baby from his arms and held him out to amaze his father.

Bereft of the infant, Jordan didn't know what to do with his hands. He clasped them behind his back, as he sometimes did when he was lecturing, and continued to pace the room. "It is perfectly clear; the ideal night for it."

"Haven't you a lecture to give?" Phoebe asked quietly.

He took another turn about the room, wishing suddenly he had not latched on to this ridiculous idea. "No. I lecture on Wednesday. There is nothing scheduled for tonight."

"So you are not nearly as busy as you pretend," Hillary said with an arch smile. "Oh don't give me that cross look, Jordan. I know you are always busy with your tutoring. I am only quizzing you."

"It is too clear a night to miss going to the observatory," he said, feeling unaccountably anxious that Phoebe might decline the strange invitation. "You have always expressed curiosity as to what I do, and so I thought I would show you."

Phoebe said nothing, only looked at him with that odd, sad expression on her face. He wondered what went on in that lovely head sometimes. Did she really believe he hadn't loved her? Did she ever wonder what life would have been like if—? He pushed the thoughts out of his head.

"Sounds amusing," said Hartfield, heaving himself out of his chair. "What do you say, Hil?"

As his brother-in-law had never evinced an interest in anything that did not involve food, drink, sports, or politics, Jordan wondered if he'd heard right. But the man was straightening his waistcoat and acting as though the matter was settled. Jordan resisted the urge to warn Hartfield that the sights to be seen at the observatory were hardly likely to amuse him.

Hillary was making indecisive noises. "Oh, but the baby is going through such a terrible time at the moment," she said, looking worriedly at the child.

"He'll cut his tooth whether you're here or not," her husband said firmly. "Give him over to his nurse and we'll go out. It will be good for you."

"But it's so late," she protested.

"Oh do come, Hillary," Phoebe put in suddenly. "It will be such great fun. And we shall learn something besides." She looked at Jordan with a slightly quizzical expression. "Perhaps we shall learn who your brother is after all."

Hillary refused to leave her long-suffering child, however, so in the end it was only Hartfield and Phoebe who walked to St. John's College. They were eyed over by the head porter at the gatehouse, but as Jordan was there to assure the man of their characters, he begrudgingly allowed them in.

The observatory was built on top of the Shrewsbury gatehouse between two inner courtyards. It was not large, just one room with windows on all sides and a large telescope occupying the center. All around the room were instruments, models, and charts.

Hartford leaned back on his heels, his chubby hands stuffed into his waistcoat pockets, and his elbows out like little wings. "Is that it?" he exclaimed, visibly disappointed. "It looks like nothing so much as an overgrown spyglass."

"It is one of the best in the country," Jordan countered, feeling slightly defensive.

"But you're stuck always looking in one direction, ain't you?" He nodded grimly, as though this observation would expose the fatal flaw in the science of astronomy.

Jordan glanced at Phoebe and saw her look up from the orrery she was examining. She had a curious expression on her face, and for some reason this pleased him enormously. He walked over to the model of the solar system and gave Jupiter a push so that she could see the moons revolve.

"We can look in any direction you please," he said, gesturing toward the windows. He walked back to the refracting telescope and pivoted it around toward the eastern window.

He felt exhilarated, excited. This was the thing he was most passionate about, and it was so hard to find people who understood the magic of it. The students were generally good, though most would go on to take up their livings or seats in the Lords and would forget everything they had learned. Some were genuinely talented and interested, and of course his fellow professors were all of the highest caliber, but—

But somehow it seemed more special to show it to Phoebe and to see her tilt her head and smile with that little quizzical look of interest.

"What are we to look at tonight?" she asked, going to a tall window and looking up into the darkness. "You must forgive my ignorance, Jordan, but I must admit that I never gave the stars very much thought." She closed her eyes and gave a laugh that was almost shy. "You must think that shocking."

He didn't of course. Most people hardly looked up, stars or no stars. He himself, who had read astronomy at Oxford when he was a student, hadn't really fallen in love with it until much later. After Phoebe had jilted him. He'd left London to bury himself in the country, and he'd rediscovered astronomy. How strange that his two loves should be here now, meeting for the first time.

"It is a whole other world," he said, gesturing toward the slates on the walls used to write out reckonings. Then he laughed, feeling unexpectedly awkward. "Well, I suppose of course it is. It's many other worlds."

Phoebe continued to look up at the sky, but she

smiled. The tilt of her chin, the curve of her mouth, they were doing strange things to him, so he busied himself carefully setting the angle of the telescope and went to shutter the lamps.

How strange that he had wanted to bring her here. Until now he had jealously guarded this sanctuary. Of course his students came for their weekly lectures, and the rest of the astronomy fellows did their own research here, but somehow he felt that it was his. Over the last nine years, he had spent countless nights here, watching the ponderous and silent dance above him. The fact that he had actually invited her here to share his private domain was surprising. But he was glad that he had.

It was dark in the observatory tower now, but Phoebe had moved to examine the star charts that papered the narrow spaces between the open windows. He was relieved; it somehow seemed more intimate in the tower when it was dark.

"It is a very special time of year," he said, trying to assume his lecturer voice. "The Lyrids, which occur every year in late April, have started. Generally, they are not terribly spectacular, nothing compared to some of the other seasonal meteor events, but this year appears to be particularly abundant."

"Meteors?" Hartfield looked nonplussed.

"Shooting stars." Phoebe came to stand beside him and look up again at the sky. She shot him a wicked look. "Only Jordan would make them sound so prosaic."

Her nearness made him want to reach out to her. He cleared his throat, which felt oddly tight. "If last night is anything to go by, it should be quite interesting. Of course, they will be at their peak in two days, which is when I will lecture on them. But to-night will give you a good look. It's a fine night, little moon, very clear."

He busied himself with focusing the telescope in the correct quadrant of the sky. Phoebe was close over his shoulder watching him. She asked questions about his every move. His wished his students were half so curious.

"How do you know this will happen?" Hartfield demanded, stumping over to the telescope. "Do you mean to say that these things just fall like clockwork? Can't predict the weather a year in advance, no mat-ter what that dashed almanac says. If you think you can predict anything else falling out of the sky, I'd say it's all humbug."

Jordan walked to the slate and began to diagram his explanation, but Hartfield stopped him. "So what happens? Crops don't grow? Strange tides?"

"No," he admitted reluctantly. "It won't affect us at all."

"Don't know why you study it then," Hartfield muttered. He peered through the eyepiece of the telescope and did not appear impressed. "I'll leave that for you longheaded fellows." He moved across the room to sit back down on a stool near the wall and began reading the newspaper by the feeble light of the dark lantern.

Jordan considered asking him not to smudge the calculations on the slate board behind him, but de-cided his brother-in-law would not suffer too much from a little chalk on the back of his coat.

"I haven't seen a shooting star since I was a child," Phoebe said, still looking intently at the sky. "It's quite hard to see the stars in London, so I suppose I got used to being without them. I know you must think that shock—oh!"—she pointed up excitedly—"I think I saw one!"

He positioned the telescope between the constellations of Lyra and Hercules, just southwest of the bright star Vega. "Yes," he said after a moment. "I'd say we'll be in for a show. Really, 1803 is turning out to be most remarkable, astronomically speaking. There's another. And there will only be more, since they peak long after midnight."

He was glad he had something to show her. It was as though the sky were showing off for her, in the most spectacular way he could have wished. He was as proud as if he had engineered it himself.

"Are they really stars?" she asked quietly, still watching the sky.

"No, they're lumps of matter, primarily metal. Iron mostly. They're far smaller than stars." He considered launching into a discussion of meteorites, but decided she was only half listening to him anyway.

"Come and take a look for yourself." He took her hand and led her to the telescope. It had been so long since he'd held her hand in the dark. He wondered if she realized she'd tightened her fingers around his. "Now, stand here and look in that just like you would a spyglass. There you go. If you need to focus the image. . . ." Her cheek brushed his shoulder as she leaned in to look. He guided her hands to the focusing mechanism. Her fingers were cool and smooth.

He realized they had both been whispering. He shot a glance at Hartfield, but the man was absorbed in reading the paper.

"Oh!" she exclaimed. "I see now. Good heavens, it's closer than I thought. There is nothing moving at the moment. I suppose I will just have to wait until another comes." She stood there, still, and he did not move away from her. "There's one. And another! Very bright."

"I counted three hundred in an hour last night," he said. "But he wasn't looking at the sky, he was noticing that she had a tiny mole on the back of her neck, near the hairline. Had he never noticed it before? There was something feminine about it. Kissable about it.

She remained silent, enraptured by the silent fireworks.

"There! Did you see that one? Oh, Jordan, did you see it? It was perfectly enormous. Oh dear, I think I bumped the telescope. It's quite off kilter now." She looked up at him and for the first time he realized how very close they stood. "Do tell me I didn't break it," she said, but her whisper quavered.

He moved in and refocused the telescope's lenses slightly. He could hear her breathing beside him. The attraction between them was so strong that the air fairly crackled with it. "Now, that should give you a good view. Try that."

He didn't mean to, he really didn't, but he kept his hand on her waist as he guided her back to the telescope. She did not object.

The telescope had been set up for a man of his height, and he felt her rise onto her toes to peer into the eyepiece. "This is the most beautiful thing I've ever seen," she said at last, still whispering.

She did not look up as she spoke, but he felt a

strange, sweet pain inside him, as though she had praised him in the strongest language. She loved what he loved. She was enraptured by the sky.

Was it his imagination, or was she leaning slightly in toward him? It was likely nothing; she was obviously intent on watching the meteors. He shot a glance at Hartfield, but the man was snoring, the paper drooping off his knees. Good. The last thing he needed was for the man to report to Hillary that he'd been making a fool of himself over Phoebe.

"That's a lot of wishes," she said, with a little laugh.

"What?"

She took her eye from the telescope and stared at him. "Are you so academic that you have forgotten that you can wish on falling stars?"

He had. He actually had. "What do you wish for?" he asked, before he realized it was a dangerous question.

She turned back toward the telescope and watched silently for so long, he wondered if she'd heard him. "I wish I had known to look for this every April. The Lyrids? Is that what they're called? I have never seen anything like this."

"This year is special," he said modestly, as though he'd had anything to do with it. "There are other, more spectacular meteor events. The Tears of St. Lawrence in August, for instance. Though this year's Lyrids outdoes them all." He heard her give a little gasp as another bright streak of light scratched the sky. Good God, but he'd never seen the April meteors this fine. In another moment, the rest of the Cambridge astronomers would be pounding on the door. But it was early yet, for astronomers; he had a few minutes more. He moved closer to her. "But what do you really wish for?"

Beneath her pelisse, he could feel her trembling. "Money," she said brazenly. "Money to pay you back."

He tightened his arm around her. "Forget about that."

"Oh?" she raised a brow without looking up from the telescope. "Then I suppose I have nothing left to wish for."

He was suddenly very serious. "Nothing?"

She remained silent for a long time. "Sometimes I wish that things had been different," she said quietly at last.

"Sometimes I do too."

She turned away from the telescope and looked at him. Her skin was palely luminous, and her eyes shiny in the dark. She had never been more beautiful.

"Anything else, Phoebe?" His fingers found the narrow hollow of her spine. She was trembling still, but she did not pull away.

Her gaze dropped to his cravat, flickered to his face, then back to his cravat again. "There was a time . . ." she began.

She was talking about the night at the opera. The night when he had kissed her. He brought his fingers under her chin and forced her to look at him. "Is that what you wish for?"

"Oh, you don't even know what I was going to say." She gave an embarrassed laugh and tried to move away, but he kept her close.

"I counted three hundred falling stars last night," he whispered. "And with every one I wished to kiss you." It wasn't true. He'd wished for far more. He'd wished that things had been different. That he had been the one to marry Phoebe years ago. That there never had been an Eleanor Whitcombe or an Arthur DeVaux.

She looked confused, and even in the dark he could tell that she was blushing. "Don't be ridiculous, Jordan," she chided. "Besides"—she gave a tiny nervous laugh—"doling out three hundred kisses would take ages."

He was genuinely embracing her now. He hadn't intended it, but she was in his arms. This would complicate things, he knew it. Wherever this led it would bring up issues that were better left undisturbed. "What do you wish for Phoebe?" he asked again.

They looked at each other for a moment, both unsure.

She rose onto her toes until she was eye to eye with him. "Let me show you," she said. And then she leaned in and kissed him.

Her mouth was just as he remembered it. But nine years ago she had been shy. Now her kiss was passionate, demanding, even. His senses reeled; he felt for a moment as though he were falling through space. He'd been playing the aggressor with no idea what had been in store. He'd barely marshaled his senses enough to kiss her back when she broke away.

She was staring at him with a wide-eyed expression. "Oh. I didn't mean to do that. I mean, I did. But I didn't expect—" She stepped back, pressing her hand to her mouth. "I never—that is—" She shot a guilty look at Hartfield, who continued to snore. "I don't know what to think. I wish—"

He kissed her again. "Wish away. We've plenty more falling stars."

"No." She disentangled herself. "You confuse me. I need to think."

He'd thought too much. Now he only wanted to feel her in his arms again. "Phoebe. Don't make this complicated. You know very well how I feel about you. I won't kiss you if you don't want me to, but please"—he clasped her hand between his own—"please, let's give what was between us another chance." There. He'd said it. Sort of.

She retrieved her hand. "It's late. We are both tired." She did not say no.

"Think on it?" God, he was begging like a schoolboy.

"I must go home. Hillary will wonder what has become of us." She did not answer his question, but she wore a small smile. There was a new look of hope about her that made him think that things might, perhaps, work out after all.

She walked toward the slumped form of Hartfield, but he held her back. "One last wish?" he teased.

"I think we've both had quite enough wishes for the moment." She shook Hillary's husband by the shoulder. "Besides," she said with a wicked light in her eye, "you said there will be many more shooting stars."

Nine

After three days of clear skies, nature decided she had exposed quite enough of her charms and settled down to rain for the next week. Phoebe sat in the front parlor, endlessly sewing the growing collection of little shirts. If Hillary's baby was obliging enough not to grow, he likely would be well outfitted in linen until he went to university.

She put down her stitching and looked out the window. The misty rain blotted out any view but the front steps. At least it had been fine for Jordan's Wednesday lecture. She hated to think that his students would miss out on seeing the Lyrids.

Lyrids. It even had a magical sound to it. She smiled to herself and pulled the thread through the cloth. Three days later and her body was still humming from Jordan's kiss. Oh it had been foolish indeed to yield to temptation, but who could have resisted under that magical rain of stars?

The house was strangely quiet. Hillary had gone to see Mrs. Lane, who, in a rare departure from schedule, had fallen ill. Hartfield was ensconced in his study, and the baby was asleep. Phoebe savored the solitude. It gave her a little time, the first in days, to think.

Of course, she realized after a few minutes, that that was the hard part. She didn't know what to think. Jordan had changed into a man she hardly knew. He was no longer the madcap young man who thought everything in life was a lark to be experienced by the DeVaux cousins. He was no longer the man who'd looked at her with brokenhearted shock when she'd announced she was to marry Arthur. But was he still the man she had once loved?

"Ridiculous," she said aloud, tying off her thread. It didn't matter who he was. It mattered who *she* was. And she was a woman who was learning to live her own life. She had worked so hard to learn economy, and it would not be long before she was released from any financial obligation to anyone.

For the first time in her life she'd be free.

His kiss had been a temptation. When he embraced her, it seemed as though all the strength went out of her. It was heady, but so dangerous. She wouldn't give up independence so fast.

But her heart skipped about as though it didn't have any notion of her firm intention. What if she and Jordan really could start over?

She folded up the little shirt and put it away in the sewing basket. She couldn't concentrate anyway. "It wasn't as though he mentioned marriage," she reminded herself. He'd only asked that they give their romance another chance. Perhaps she was naïve, or vain, or both. Could she enjoy a mere dalliance with Jordan?

The idea made her nearly laugh aloud. Of course she could not. Another kiss like the one in the observatory, and she would be head over heels in love with him again.

She didn't mean to, she really didn't, but somehow she found herself imagining what it would be like to live in a little house like this one with Jordan. To show him the household accounts, exalt over their own children's teeth, and walk out at night to wish on the stars.

She gave herself a mental shake. Impossible. A liaison with Jordan, of any kind, would not suit her plans.

A part of her brain though was still thinking about falling stars.

There was the sound of footsteps running up the walk. A figure leapt up the steps in a bound and began pounding on the front door.

She had gotten up to look out the window to see who it was when the man burst into the room.

"Boxty!" she exclaimed, looking at the disheveled man dripping water on the Axminster. "What is amiss?"

"Where is Professor DeVaux?" he demanded without preamble.

She led him over to the fire. As she helped him out of his greatcoat, she saw that there was a paper clutched in his fist. The rain had streaked the ink but it was obvious that it bore Jordan's name and direction. "I don't know," she replied. "He has not been here in days." A tight knot of fear formed in her stomach. "Has something happened to him?"

Boxty looked at her as though he were seeing her for the first time. "Oh," he said, "I thought you were Mrs. Hartfield for a moment. Is she here? I need to find Professor DeVaux."

"Did you check his rooms at the college?" she asked, though she knew, of course, that he would have.

He nodded, still looking distracted. "Checked everywhere. Urgent message. Must find him."

"What has happened?" she asked again. "Is it something I can help you with?"

He flapped the sodden paper in front of her. "William is ill. Very ill."

"William?" she repeated, bewildered.

"The boy from Bedfordshire," the student replied cryptically. "I hadn't seen the professor in days, and you know I am to have my tutoring session with him today. While I was waiting for him outside his chambers, an express came so I paid for it, of course. Had to; it was an express," he assured her, his sandy brows high on his forehead.

Boxty began pacing the room, leaving a trail of wet footprints. "It said urgent on it, quite bold-like, and I wondered if it might say where the professor was, since I'd waited three-quarters of an hour and there was no sign of him." He ran his hand through his hair. "I know I shouldn't have opened his letter, but, well, dash it all, I was worried and so I see I should have been, because he must go to the child!"

The roiling inside her grew more violent. Boxty wasn't making sense, but any more questions would only disturb him further. She kept her face serene and put her arm through the young man's. "Come, Boxty, let me get my cloak. We'll find Professor

DeVaux." She pulled the bell and drew him into the entryway. "Is he lecturing at this hour?"

"No, he's supposed to be tutoring me."

Boxty's obvious panic was eating away at her own calm. "Did he mention any appointments? You must think back."

He made an impatient gesture. "No, no I would have remembered. He never misses our sessions."

"Have you looked at the observatory?"

He squinted slightly and thought for a moment. "It's daytime. And it's raining. Why would he be there?"

Phoebe dragged on her cloak and took up her umbrella. "I don't know. I just thought that since he isn't in his rooms, and he isn't here . . ."

He uncrumpled the letter, read it again with a worried expression, and then shoved it into his greatcoat pocket as he put the dripping article back on. "Very well. Let's look there." He looked stricken. "I shouldn't have read the letter, I know. But I worried that—"

She laid her hand on his arm. "I know you only opened it because you were worried, and I'm certain Jordan won't mind." They went out into the rain. It was coming down steadily now, a thick, misty rain that seemed to wet everything instantly. The street was cleft with rivulets of mud and the sidewalk was little better. They huddled under the umbrella and slogged toward the St. John's College observatory.

"Quite wet," she said, hoping to start a conversation with Boxty, who was looking as though he might clench his jaw to powder.

He said nothing, just looked vaguely into the sky,

as though this were the first time he'd noticed the bruised clouds.

"I'm certain we'll find him," she tried again. "And then he'll set everything aright."

Boxty merely grunted and pulled his foot out of the quagmire at the curb.

She was concerned for the boy. He was overreacting entirely. Whatever was the trouble, Jordan was perfectly capable of taking care of it. "Is this boy from Bedfordshire a student of the professor's?" she asked.

Boxty looked at her with an expression of surprise. " 'Course not. He's the professor's son." And then, mistaking her blank look for confusion, "Lady Whitcombe's son."

She stumbled and Boxty caught her by the elbow before she fell. "Lady Whitcombe's son," she echoed in a hollow voice.

The young man looked alarmed. "You didn't know? Oh! Oh no. I wouldn't have said anything—I thought everyone knew." His face pinched in an expression of misery. "Of course it isn't the thing one talks about, but everyone knew. He keeps them somewhere in Bedfordshire. Don't know where exactly. A cottage near Potton, I believe."

The world had fallen out from under her. Without Boxty's hand on her arm, she would have sat down in the mud.

Jordan and Eleanor Whitcombe had a child together.

On the day they'd gone boating, he'd tried to protest that there had been nothing between him and Lady Whitcombe. The liar. Oh she'd seen them that day, true enough. But that hadn't been the honest reason she had ended their engagement. Dear God, if she hadn't . . .

She was going to humiliate herself by casting up her accounts in the street. A child with Lady Whitcombe. And then—"He did not marry her?" she heard herself say.

Somehow they had reached the steps to the observatory. She couldn't go in. She couldn't see him.

Boxty was looking more worried than ever. "Oh dear, I've shocked you. I'm so sorry. I didn't know you didn't know."

Whatever expression she was wearing seemed to alarm him further. "Don't think badly of him, Lady DeVaux. He couldn't marry her. She was already married. Lord Whitcombe would not grant her a divorce when he was alive, and he's only been dead less than a year. The professor couldn't marry her before her year's mourning was up, now could he?"

Lady Whitcombe and Jordan had a child. Her vision was going dark around the edges.

"And I know that you are thinking that perhaps the professor should have gone down and lived with them in Potton, or wherever they are," Boxty was continuing. "And I must admit that I don't really know why he doesn't but it seems to me that if that was what Lady Whitcombe wanted, he would have done it because you and I both know the professor, and we know that he would always do the right thing."

She couldn't really follow what Boxty was saying. And she certainly didn't know anything for certain anymore. Heavens, she'd been well on her way to falling in love with him again. She'd thought they had another chance. She had thought of marriage! How naïve to have talked herself into believing he wished for something honorable.

At that moment the door to the spiral staircase leading to the observatory was flung open and Jordan careened into them.

"Oh, Fuller," he exclaimed, "I just recalled our meeting. The Lyrids, you know. This year is most unusual. Historic! I've been meeting with the other astronomy fellows. You must forgive me. I was—" He broke off and stared at Phoebe. He looked tired, harried, badly shaved. His neckcloth had twisted around to one side and his hair fell over his eyes. "Phoebe." His voice was warm with emotion as he smiled. "I'm so—"

"Will is ill," Boxty interrupted. "There was an express from Lady Whitcombe. You must go to her immediately."

Phoebe's last thread of hope was snapped. Instead of looking confused and asking what the devil Boxty was talking about, Jordan's brows drew together in immediate concern. "Is she at home?" he demanded. "Give me the letter. Good God, why didn't she write earlier? It could be too late now."

Boxty thrust the letter into his hands. "Shall I hire you a carriage or will you ride?"

He looked over the letter, his mouth tightening into a grim line. "I'll ride. Yes. I'll go now." He looked at Phoebe, but no longer seemed to see her. "Thank you for bringing this to me. I should have been at home to receive it. I've been"—he seemed to search for a word, his tired brown eyes unfocused—"thinking."

Boxty started talking about changing horses and

the number of hours it would take to get to Potton.
The two of them walked back toward Trinity, oblivious
of the rain, in rapid discussion. Phoebe stood on the
steps to the observatory and watched them go.

Ten

Every night the next week she dreamed of Arthur. This morning when Phoebe awoke, the sheets were tangled around her legs and a cold sweat had formed along her hairline. It wasn't a dream she wanted to remember. She slid out of bed, glad to be awake. It was early, too early even for Annie to be about, so she dressed herself and went downstairs.

As she had done every day since she had discovered the shocking truth, she awakened to a heavy sense of dread. Sometimes, if she tried very hard, she could make it all the way through breakfast before she really started thinking about it.

Today, however, it attacked her at the foot of the stairs. Jordan had gone to Potton to be with Eleanor Whitcombe and his child. His family. She went into the sitting room and curled up in the chintz chair by the drawing room hearth. Last night's ashes lay in a fluffy gray pile on the grate. It was cold, but she didn't have the energy to make a fire. Not even Cook was stirring yet.

A child.

She wondered what the boy looked like. Did he have Jordan's eyes? Did he know his father was traipsing around Cambridge allowing himself to be kissed by some poor fool from his past? How humiliating that memory was. She'd flung herself at him, wantonly, convinced that he cared about her. Just like she'd believed he had nine years ago.

She'd felt guilty all those years. She'd thought she had wounded him by breaking their engagement. But he'd been unfaithful to her all along.

The sun was shooting painful lances of light over the windowsill, so she went up to draw the curtains. The dregs of yesterday's clouds were still smeared across the sky.

Fine. Things were over with Jordan. They had never *not* been over. But she was a grown woman now, not some heartbroken chit who thought the world was at an end just because someone had disappointed her. She would make her own future.

She opened up the little account book Hillary had given her and examined her finances. Nearly six weeks in Cambridge. That was only two months' rent received from the small farm in Sussex. But with her widow's portion and the interest from her shares on the 'change, she was doing all right. Not enough to pay Jordan back yet. But it wouldn't take forever. And then she could go back to London.

She tried to picture herself living, perhaps with a paid companion, in some modest rooms in a respectable, but not too fashionable part of town. A life of muslin drapes instead of silk, and a lamp on the table instead of wax candles. Her future would be simple and likely rather dull. No balls or gaming or fashionable society, but perhaps, at last, a little freedom, and a little peace.

She went to the window and peered out the slit

between the curtains. The sun was warming the stone facades of the university buildings. It was still wet from a week of rain, but the day was promising to make a better effort today.

Cambridge was all right, really. Not as mad dashing as London, but perhaps that wasn't a bad thing. Perhaps she wouldn't go back to London after all. It might be nice to live somewhere like this.

Of course not here exactly. She would leave here, and leave Jordan, just as soon as she had the capital to do so.

"Lady DeVaux!" Anne exclaimed, clutching her cap to her head. "You gave me such a fright. I went to clean your grate, and you were gone. I thought for certain you'd been carried off. But here you are. And no fire at all in here. What are you doing sitting down here in the dark with no fire? You should have rung, milady."

Phoebe gave her a chastened look. "I'm sorry. I merely awoke early and didn't quite know what to do with myself."

"Well no wonder you woke early. You went to bed directly after you got home from Mrs. Lane's yesterday afternoon. I've been worried you were taking ill. You looked so white." Her hand flew to her mouth in a gesture of surprise. "I even forgot to tell you about the box."

"What box?"

"I'm sorry I forgot, ma'am. It's just that you didn't look like you were up to thinking about anything yesterday. A box arrived for you, yesterday afternoon. A big one. From London. From Mssrs. Fielding, Hampshire, Fig and Browne."

Phoebe wrinkled her nose. "Oh. The solicitors. Nothing of interest I'd warrant."

The maid scampered out of the room and came staggering back in with a large wooden crate. "It looks so exciting. And it has your husband's name on it. Do you think they found something of his that now belongs to you? Maybe it's something valuable."

She knew Arthur well enough to know that anything of value he owned would have been converted to cash long ago and sacrificed on the baize altar.

She was mildly curious, but she didn't particularly wish to reveal any secrets in front of Annie, so she ignored the box until the girl reluctantly left the room.

The box was latched but not locked and inside was a letter from Mr. Fig explaining that the tenants of the town house had found this box full of the late Lord DeVaux's effects, and not knowing her whereabouts, had sent it to him.

Below that looked to be nothing but letters and bills. She sifted through them, tempted to simply close the lid or cast the whole thing on the fire. She did not wish to remember her husband as nothing but a wastrel. There had been a better side, at least in the early years. Farther down, letters began appearing in a different hand. She examined them more closely.

They were love letters. To Arthur.

She let out a strangled laugh. Of course she wasn't too terribly surprised. Arthur had lost interest in her quickly enough. She'd always suspected he'd had a ladybird. But these letters were from someone well educated, not a common fancy piece. They were signed "N."

The next layer was from someone who wrote on pink hot-pressed paper with a round and childish hand. Below that, several from someone named Kitty. Besides her obvious lack of spelling ability, Kitty certainly had a vivid way of expressing her desires. Phoebe blushed and put those letters aside. Below that were letters in elegant copperplate from a lady who signed her missives with a symbol of a heart.

Phoebe didn't look further. It was painful, even though she wasn't surprised. She could not resist peeking back at the dates on a few of the letters, just to ascertain exactly when the affairs had been taking place. Was she really so blind that she hadn't been aware of what was going on so blatantly under her nose? Was the Lady D Kitty mentioned so mockingly herself?

She wondered if the whole *ton* had been laughing at her all along. Poor Phoebe DeVaux. Married to the biggest whoremonger in Town.

Now of course, she couldn't shut off her mind if she'd wanted to. N. Who was N? Nell Highbridge? Possibly. She had counted Nell a friend, but she had noticed that her visits stopped abruptly when Arthur died. Would Nell have done that to her?

She thought of the funeral. How many of those weeping women were crying over their lost lover? And stupid Phoebe, thinking the whole world sympathetic.

Annie came into the room, clucking solicitously. "Here's your tea, milady. Oh, I didn't mean to startle you." She looked taken aback when Phoebe slammed shut the lid to the box. The girl opened her mouth, looked at Phoebe for a moment, then closed it. "Just ring for me if you need anything, ma'am," she said at last. She cast a last lingeringly curious glance at the box and left the room.

Phoebe stared at the box. Hateful thing. And why now, this ugly twist of the knife? Jordan didn't love her; he never had. It had been foolish to harbor hopes in that direction. But was it so much to ask that one's husband love you? And not everyone else's wife instead? At last she opened the box again and began slowly feeding the letters into the fire.

When she had finished, she got up and brushed off her gown, then rang for Annie.

The girl appeared so quickly that it was obvious she'd been hovering nearby. "Are you well, milady?" she exclaimed. "You look very pale!"

"Not at all. I'm quite all right." She forced her mouth into a smile. "I had a slight headache, but now it's quite gone."

Annie looked skeptical. "You still look peaky. I'll warrant it's on account of this dratted rain. It will be better today, but my mother always says that any change in the weather brings on the headache and all her rheumatics." She narrowed her eyes at Phoebe. "I'd say the headache's not quite gone."

"Don't be silly," she said, resisting the sudden urgent need to rub her tense brow. "I know exactly what will make me feel just the thing. I shall go for a brisk walk along the river."

Annie's expression was forced into one of tepid enthusiasm. "I'll get our coats, milady."

"Oh don't be silly. It's far too early for anyone to be about. I can go quite properly on my own." The prim notion of taking a maid everywhere one went was quite properly ignored for the most part in sleepy Cambridge.

"Oh no, I shall go with you, ma'am," Annie insisted, with a look so sincere that Phoebe knew the maid was convinced she meant to throw herself into the Cam or some such ridiculous thing.

As though a little disappointment over the DeVaux cousins was worth anything dramatic. A cruel part of her mind flung up a picture of Jordan, back in the days when she had first fallen in love with him, holding Eleanor Whitcombe in his arms. And kissing Eleanor like he had kissed her that night in the observatory. "Nonsense," she said brusquely. "You were complaining of a sore throat yesterday, Annie, and the last thing you need is to be out-of-doors. I shan't go far, and I'll be back before breakfast."

Annie looked doubtful, but the damp fog that blotted the rising sun settled the question. In the end, Phoebe put on her warmest blue wool pelisse and braved the early morning alone.

Nature evidently had decided that spring was too much of an effort and had reverted to a wettish gloom. The countryside across the river was a uniformly depressing grayish brown, and not even the new green of the fields seemed to cheer it. It was hard to believe that a few weeks ago it had been warm enough to punt along the river. A false spring. She walked on, refusing to draw parallels with her own life.

It was early, the delicate mists not yet burnt off by the sun. The river had exhaled a heavy fog, that drifted over the backs. There was no sound but the occasional lowing of the cows that grazed by the banks.

Phoebe found her favorite flat rock and sat down, watching King's College's chapel coalesce out of the mist. It was her favorite of all the chapels in the university. She'd seen them all, pestering the rectors for details of their dates and details. Reverend Hastings had taken her under his wing and consented to walk with her nearly every day to new areas of the university. She'd become quite a familiar sight around the colleges.

The chapel lumbered out of the fog, graceful and solid at the same time.

She heared a steady splashing down the river and waited patiently until at last a punt appeared. The man poling it was alone, and looked extremely intent on the exercise. She smiled at his serious expression.

"Hello, Boxty," she called out as he passed.

Boxty nearly capsized the boat as he started. "Lady DeVaux! What are you doing here? It's a bit early to be out, wouldn't you say?"

"I would indeed."

He scowled, even as he poled the boat to her side of the bank. "You should be at home, not walking about on your own."

"I am not on my own. You are here now." She smiled. "And as for being at home, why are you out and about?"

He looked at bit sheepish. "Couldn't sleep. Bit anxious I suppose. Thought the air might clear my head." He drove the pole into the soft mud and hooked an arm around it. "I haven't seen you in an age. Why do you not come out with us? I stopped by yesterday to see if you wished to accompany us on a pleasure outing to Newmarket, but Mrs. Hartfield said you were out."

She threw a small pebble into the river, listening for the satisfying plunk as it dropped into the water. "I've been keeping myself busy," she said with a shrug. "I thought I would try to read a bit more."

Boxty's expression was something between awe and guilt. "Reading?"

"Well, I realized I'd spent much of my time in London doing nothing. I don't mean to say one has to spend all of one's time doing things that are meaningful, but I didn't want to look back on my life and realize that I'd done nothing more than go to parties and change my clothes."

Boxty looked slightly bewildered. "Are you a blue-stocking?" he asked, in a voice of deep suspicion.

She laughed. "Of course not. I'm not clever enough. But I have been going to the circulating library to read. I enjoy it. I don't pretend to study or to be doing anything particularly lofty, but I do enjoy it."

"Why do I never see you?" he asked.

She opened her mouth to answer when Boxty interrupted her with a laugh. "If you've been hiding in the library, you know I should never find you. But that isn't what I meant. I mean, I never see you at Trinity. I used to see you there with Mr. Hartfield or with Professor DeVaux, but it's been nearly a week since I've seen you at all."

She didn't wish to tell him she'd been avoiding Trinity's grounds. And even so she lived in fear she would run into Jordan. She watched for him everywhere. Dreading, and at the same time wishing to see him.

She didn't want to ask Boxty if Jordan was back from Bedfordshire. Hillary hadn't mentioned it, but with the baby's recent colic, Jordan's sister hardly had time to mention anything but lengthy and detailed updates on the child's health.

Phoebe threw another stone into the river and tried to think of something to say. "How are your studies?"

Boxty grimaced. "Well enough. I suppose. Oh I don't know. I can't seem to care about being bookish now that Professor DeVaux isn't around to make certain things stick in my head."

She couldn't help it. She really couldn't. "Is he not back then?" Her voice sounded tight and squeaky.

Boxty leaned his head against the pole. "Comes back today or tomorrow, I think. He's got to. Got to lecture. Professor Hillyard from St. John's did it last week, but I must say, he's just dreadful. He lectures in astronomy too, you know, but everyone knows he's a dead bore. And he must be well near a hundred years old now. Kept referring to George Atwood as a brilliant young man and Lord knows *he's* got to be sixty."

Phoebe fought back the pictures in her mind. Jordan and his son. And the woman who was not his wife. Did Lady Whitcombe wish to be married to Jordan? She was free of her husband now. She could marry whomever she liked. Phoebe felt the familiar knot of unhappiness form in her stomach.

Boxty's sigh brought her back from her thoughts. "You're a clever one, Lady DeVaux. Perhaps *you* can help me."

He looked so anxious and sad that she instantly felt very selfish for concentrating only on her own little woes. "Of course, Boxty. I'm happy to help you if I can."

"I hate it here."

She looked at him in surprise. "Do you? I thought you said you liked Cambridge."

He shrugged, leaning on the pole and pressing his cheek to it in an exaggerated expression of despondency. "Oh, I like Cambridge well enough, I suppose. It is the university part I detest. I mean, I like Professor DeVaux of course. But not the studying. You won't tell the professor, will you? He'd be so disappointed in me. Just like m'parents."

Phoebe pulled up a blade of grass and rolled it between her fingers. Poor Boxty. He did everything to please people. He was like a big clumsy puppy with no thought other than to gain the approval of those around him. While he was surrounded with people quite happy to tell him what he *should* do, no one had ever really asked him what he *wanted* to do. "Have you thought about leaving the university?"

"Of course," he said quickly. "But I can't. My father says I can't until I manage to get my degree. Which is ridiculous. Everyone knows a university education is less than useless for someone in my position. Most fellows with titles don't have one. It's only for clerics and barristers. Can't see what good the thing would do me." He scratched his chin. "Particularly since I'm not clever."

"Then why does he insist on it?" she asked.

Boxty thought on this for a moment. "Because he suffered through it, I suppose. Because he thinks it will keep me out of trouble in Town, more likely. Oh but I'd so much rather be anywhere than here." He looked utterly despairing for a moment. "I mean, Professor DeVaux is grand, and some of the lads are a laugh, and of course you . . . but it's all the studying. I hate it. And I shall never be able to leave."

"Have you written to your family? To tell them how you really feel? I'm certain they would be understanding if they knew."

Boxty's sheepish expression made him look like a little boy. "It's the professor I'm worried about."

"Why?"

"He's invested so much time. Given me so much extra attention. . . ." He trailed off, looking helpless. "He would be very disappointed in me. And, well, he's more like a father to me than my real father. The trouble is," he said glumly, "that I'll disappoint him if I leave, and disappoint him if I stay, because I'll never be able to finish. He's just going to be more and more disappointed in me."

She stared into the distance, digesting this. It was hard to imagine Jordan forcing someone, particularly his favorite student, to do something he didn't want. But then, Jordan was only acting in what he thought was Boxty's best interests. Obviously the man had many faults, but he took his role as a teacher seriously. "What would you prefer to be doing?" she asked.

Boxty's face split into a wide grin. "Everything. I'd like to do the grand tour, see Egypt, Switzerland, all that. I'd like to go to London, though in general I don't like London. But I'd like to see White's and the opera and learn to box at Cribb's and see St. Paul's."

"See St. Paul's?" she echoed. It hardly seemed like an ordinary ambition of a lively young man.

"Well, I've seen it from the outside, of course. I

mean, my parents live in London. Seen it loads of times. But I've never been inside. When Lord and Lady Warwickshire go to church, they go to St. George's, certainly not St. Paul's."

"It's a lovely building," she agreed.

"Yes. And quite a revolution in architecture for its time." He nodded vigorously. "There's nothing like it anywhere. Of course I'd like to see the grand architecture in Rome and Paris and all, but I think I'd like to start with St. Paul's."

"Why did you not study architecture, instead of astronomy?" she asked.

Boxty looked at her as though she were a lunatic. "Architecture? That's not a proper course of study. It's not in the *quadrivium*, anyway."

She shrugged and threw another stone into the river. "If you think it is interesting, I think you should pursue it."

He looked thoughtful, but not very convinced. "Wish I could study whatever I liked. I used to know a great deal about architecture. I suppose I liked our library and it went from there. I don't know enough to actually become an architect, of course. Don't have the head for numbers to do that. But I do rather like it. I suppose you've seen King's chapel?"

Boxty was something of a dullard in academics, by his own admission, but when he was interested in something it was quite a different matter. "I have," she said with a smile, "but certainly not with someone who knew so much about it as you. Would you show it to me?"

Boxty tied up the boat and leapt out. The fog had cleared, and it was only a short walk to the chapel steps. The rector let them in, looking them over with a suspicious eye.

She'd seen Kings Chapel before, during her rambles through the university, but it was always breathtaking. High above their heads rose a series of arches, each one splaying webs of ribbing into the other. It seemed impossible that so much stone could be held up so high.

"It's really remarkable," Boxty whispered, though there was no one in the place. "They're dead proud of it, the lads at King's, so you hate to praise it. But it is very fine."

"It looks like spun sugar," she said, craning her neck to see the lacy vaults that fanned overhead. They walked through the nave in silence. The early morning light that filtered through the panes of glass from the enormous windows was a pale gold. It was not really a restful place, certainly nothing like the modest country church she'd attended growing up in Somerset, nor was it like the ponderous and grave St. George, where the fashionable attended services in London. No, here the grandeur, the impressiveness of scale gave one more awe than peace.

Between the antechapel and the choir, there was a screen made up of dark wood with Tudor roses. Boxty examined it minutely. "See, H and A. Henry and Anne. Anne Boleyn of course. One of the few relics of their marriage." He pointed to the twined initials.

Another marriage that never should have happened, Phoebe mused. How peculiar that now, for the first time, she was able to voice to herself what she'd known for a long time. She never should have married Arthur. At the time she'd thought she'd had little choice. But of course she had. It didn't matter now, of course. However there was a strange freedom in being able to stop pretending that they'd loved each other.

Her thoughts naturally moved in the direction of another relationship, one that did not end in marriage. But she could not think of Jordan, Eleanor Whitcombe, and their child. She couldn't.

She and Boxty stood looking up at the screen for a long moment. "I was thinking," Boxty said at last, "about what you said last month."

"When?" At the serious expression on his face, she felt a sudden frisson of alarm that she had said something foolish about Jordan.

"When we had our picnic down by the river," he clarified, pulling at his cravat. "Do you remember? The picnic with Grinny and Joxer and Mad Jack's terrifying sister? She threw herself at me later, you know. Had to turn her off. Most embarrassing."

She remembered the day vividly. It was the day Jordan had asked why she had broken their engagement. How ridiculous. Why had he brought that up after all these years? Why could it possibly matter? Particularly when it was clear, now more than ever, that his own heart had been otherwise engaged.

Her sense of dread grew. Was it that obvious then how she felt about Jordan? Had she made a fool of herself by letting her emotions show? "What did I say?"

"That you wanted to move back to London, but that you couldn't because you didn't have enough money."

She relaxed. "Oh, well. I don't know. Perhaps I

won't go back to London. Perhaps somewhere else."
A town like Cambridge. But without Jordan.

Boxty rubbed his nose violently, and pulled again
at his neck cloth. "And I was thinking about what
else you said."

"What?" she asked, when she realized he needed
to be prompted to go on.

"That you wouldn't . . . er . . . that you wouldn't
ever . . . that is, that you wouldn't marry again," he
finished at last.

She stared at him in mild confusion while he
blushed.

He looked around the empty chapel. "I was thinking that, well, I have money and you don't," he whispered. "And I'd go to London if *you* wanted to. I've
no interest in finishing my studies you know. I wasn't
cut out for it. Shouldn't have started in the first
place. So I thought, though of course you don't have
to, I thought we might make a kind of arrangement."

The heavy incense in the chapel must have dulled
her senses. "An arrangement?"

Boxty took a deep breath and exhaled loudly. "I
thought we could marry."

A file of choirboys came in through the back of
the chapel, their shrill fighting and laughter merci-
fully filling the silence.

"Oh, Boxty . . ."

"You don't have to make up your mind now," he
interrupted, craning his neck to glare at the boys.
"Just thought I would suggest it. Get you back to
London, you know. Get me out of here. My father
couldn't possibly expect me to finish my studies if I

were married. And of course you know I think the world of you." For the first time his eyes met hers.

"I can't, Boxty."

"You don't have to answer now."

She drew a breath. "I am answering now. I must say no." She took his arm to be certain he was listening. "And it isn't because I don't care for you. I do. I just, well . . . It wouldn't be the right thing to do." Boxty deserved a love match. He shouldn't be eternally shackled to a woman who could never return his affection in the way he deserved.

"Oh," Boxty said in a flat voice. "Are you certain?"

"Yes. Thank you for the kind offer, though." She turned away from the screen and pretended to watch the boys in their miniature surplices take their places in the loft. "But I'm afraid we wouldn't suit at all."

She realized with lowering clarity that no one would ever suit. Because, despite it all, she would always be in love with Jordan.

Eleven

Jordan sat and watched the couple talk, their heads bent close together in the golden light of the chapel. What he had first taken for an intimate moment had obviously gone awry. Fuller's animated gestures had turned to sulking and then to a depressed kind of resolution and then he had gone.

Phoebe continued to sit, still and quiet, as though she were intent on becoming part of the pew by the Tudor screen. The choir practice had come and gone and then the regular Wednesday morning service. And still she sat.

She never turned back to look at him, and he was glad. He would have felt like an idiot trying to explain why he had spent half the morning watching her. He felt like he'd been slowly going mad, so perhaps this was the final manifestation of it. Walking across the backs, he'd seen Phoebe and Fuller enter the chapel and without a qualm of conscience, he'd followed them.

He'd ignored the fact that Phoebe and Fuller were obviously in private conversation and made up some cracked story in his head about how it would only be polite to say hello to her after having been gone so long.

Perhaps it was pure nosiness that had kept him lurking at the back of the chapel. He'd stopped being jealous of Fuller long ago. He could admit now that that was what that early emotion had been. He'd known how much Fuller admired Phoebe, but it had become obvious that Phoebe thought of the boy with nothing but friendship. Jordan had accompanied them on enough outings to know that Phoebe was in far more danger of being embarrassed by unwanted advances from he himself than from Fuller.

He saw the rector coming up the aisle for the third time. The man had been making helpful harrumphing noises for the last hour, obviously hoping to encourage him either to unburden his heart through confession or else get out of his chapel.

It was Phoebe he needed to unburden his heart to. What must she think of him?

"I'm going, I'm going," he grumbled, getting up and turning to go. At the last minute, he hesitated, then turned on his heel and walked quickly up the aisle to where Phoebe sat.

"I'm going, I'm going," she said irritably, gathering up her wrap and reticule without looking up.

"They will be charging you rent soon," he said with a smile.

She froze, then her head snapped up. Her expression was something close to horror. Then, her mouth closed, and she straightened her shoulders.

Already this was not going as planned. It had been madness from the start. He felt his smile growing stiff. "How are you?" he asked, barely getting the words out through teeth that suddenly refused to unclench.

"I'm very well. And you?"

"Yes, very well. Thank you."

They stood in silence for a moment. He wanted to pour out an explanation, but somehow it was stuck in his throat. She was looking at him as though he had pinned a dead rat to his lapel.

"Are you waiting for someone?" he asked, just to fill the maw of silence.

"No. I was just looking at the architecture."

He squinted up at the ceiling for a moment. "Yes. It's quite impressive. I understand why you've defected." He smiled slightly at her look of bewilderment. "Of course, as a relation of a fellow at Trinity, you're expected to think our own chapel the finest in every respect. However, in the face of such grandeur, I can see why you were seduced."

It was an unfortunate choice of words. They both knew it. It was ridiculous to pretend that nothing was wrong. Everything was wrong. Starting with the kiss in the observatory. And ending with his racing wildly off to Bedfordshire with no explanation. God knew what she'd heard since then.

"Come for a walk with me," he said, almost pleading. "There's a great deal we should talk about."

Phoebe hesitated for so long he thought that his heart would never start beating again. Then at last, she inclined her chin.

The day, which had been so fragile when they'd entered the chapel, was now bright and windy with the sun blazing at full force. He shaded his eyes and waited while she tied her bonnet. So many words were flying about in his head that he wondered how he would ever capture enough to make an explanation.

They really shouldn't be wandering about alone. He'd had enough ribbing from Caldwell and the other Trinity fellows to know that he'd already paid Phoebe too much attention in the past. He should lead her back to Hillary's house, not over the river toward the solitude of the avenue of trees that ran across the backs toward Burrell's Field. But this conversation would be difficult enough without trying to compress the story into the brief seconds of privacy they would get going through town.

She followed him obediently, but said nothing. The coolness in her manner was palpable, but what had he expected?

"I saw you with Fuller," he said, unsure where to start.

She sighed, twisting her gloves. "Poor Boxty. I have disappointed him I'm afraid. I feel very badly for him. He's such a kind and generous boy, and he could shine somewhere else."

Boy. She'd called him a boy. For some reason he felt a little better. "If he'd only apply himself . . ."

She turned on him, her pale brows drawn together in annoyance. "Academic pursuits are not everything. You live here in your tiny intellectual world, and you think that speaking in Latin and knowing the course of the stars makes one worthy as a person. Boxty isn't clever, and to you, therefore, he's a lesser kind of human being. You think you're doing him a favor to drag him kicking through every course. You should let him get sent down. He would be happier."

She looked him up and down with an expression of utter scorn. "Has it ever occurred to you that it doesn't matter?" she spat out. "Your knowledge is not helping anyone. You have not done anything for mankind with your stupid star watching."

He tightened his jaw to keep from responding. Of course she was right. When one really considered the matter with a lorgnette, his life's work did not matter. It mattered to the world of science. It mattered for the greater good. But for the immediate future?

Perhaps his world had become too small. He felt a painful emptiness edged with anger at her cruel assertion.

Ridiculously, he realized, he thought he'd impressed her. He thought his nobility, his ability to rise above those days of London scandal, his success here at Cambridge; he thought that had made her admire him. Just a little. Now he realized she still thought him a wastrel, only now one sporting a useless education.

"I'm sorry you feel that way," he said quietly.

She made an impatient gesture. "Of course you can easily respond that what I do with my life is less than useless. I've lived a profligate and lazy life, doing a great deal more harm than good." She walked on for a moment, obviously absorbed in her own thoughts. "I believe we were talking about Boxty."

Of course they were only talking about Boxty to keep from talking about Eleanor. "I like Lord Fuller very much," he said, hoping to avoid for as long as possible the discussion to come.

She made a dismissive noise with her tongue and shook her head. "You pity him. He follows you around worshiping the ground you walk on and you pity him. He is a thousand times the man you are."

He stopped and looked down at her. He knew

she'd be angry but he hadn't expected to discuss his relationship with Boxty Fuller, of all people. "At your generous and perceptive suggestion, I assure you I shall endeavor to treat the young man with every respect he deserves." He gave her a short bow and turned to go, but her hand on his arm stopped him.

"I'm sorry. I'm overwrought. You've always been most kind to Boxty and I shouldn't have implied otherwise." She gave him a small smile that somehow made her look even more sad. Her hand remained on his sleeve.

"What has happened to make you overwrought?" he asked quietly, ignoring the tingles that danced down his arm. Good God, it was happening again. He only had to look at her and he desired her. He was no better than an undergraduate lusting after the barmaid. But he had kissed that mouth, and no matter what cruel words came out of it, he wanted to kiss it now.

"Boxty"—she shook her head—"I don't know why I should be defending him, when it's him I'm upset with. He can be a great fool at times."

"Though I hear he's a thousand times the man I am," Jordan murmured.

He kept his expression neutral, even when her hand dropped to her side. "Don't be dreadful." She sighed. "I've had a wretched week."

Her eyes flicked to his. The tension between them was a tangible thing. She was asking him why he went to Bedfordshire, and he was not sure what to say. Then she dropped her gaze. There was a look of misery on her face that made him long to draw her into his arms. But he couldn't. Whatever she had heard while he was gone, she must despise him.

"Anything I can help you with?" he asked quietly.

He thought for a moment that there were tears in her eyes, but she laughed and turned away before he could be sure. "No, no. It is all silliness. Boxty has asked me to marry him, and I said no and now he's in a sulk."

He felt an unexpected stab of jealousy. Proposed? How dare the boy be so presumptuous! Of course he admired Phoebe, but he . . . Didn't he know . . . Did Fuller mean to steal her right from under his nose? "You said no," he repeated, just to be certain.

"Of course. Though I have to admit, I was very nearly tempted." Her chin went up. "He is not happy here, and I am not happy here, and he made a very compelling argument that he wanted nothing more than to go to London to set up housekeeping."

There were unpleasant prickles across his back. "And who better to show him how to spend his money in London?" he said, teasing.

She looked as though he'd slapped her. Her face grew as red as though he had.

He stopped walking and took her by the arm to force her to look at him. "I shouldn't have said that," he said. He'd done it to pique her. Because she'd wounded him. How childish. "I know you've made great efforts to learn about economy. Hillary told me she's been teaching you how to keep the household accounts."

To his dismay she looked even more insulted. "She should not have told you that."

"She is proud of you. And I am impressed that

you would make such an effort." He could see that she was struggling against her fury and humiliation, and he hated himself for inflicting both. "I know that makes me sound like a great prude, and I don't mean to say that you should have changed in any way, but I am very glad that you have taken steps to take control of your life." He'd said it all wrong, but he hoped she knew what he meant.

She was looking up at him, her green eyes filled with an emotion he could not read. He had not released her and she did not pull away from him.

"We are both saying unkind things we do not mean. It has been a difficult week for us both."

The silence grew long, and he realized he was staring at her with an intent expression that must be most daunting. He let her go and resumed walking. Good God, would she always have this hold on him? Perhaps he should have encouraged her to marry Boxty. It would be better to get her out of here. It was madness to keep the powder keg so near the open flame of his desire.

"How was your trip?" she asked in a tight voice, daring him to answer.

He drew a deep breath. It was time to tell her. After all, that's what he'd planned to do. "Phoebe, let us drop all roundaboutation. I don't know what you know, and I am certain I appeared very much like a madman the day I left for Bedfordshire."

She was waiting patiently, not offering to help. He could see the tense muscle in her jaw.

"I went to Potton . . ." Was there any tale he could spin to make this sound better? Would he be able to go through with it?

"Yes?" she drew out the word impatiently.

"I went to see Lady Whitcombe." Good God but this was hellish. "The wife of the man who killed Arthur."

"Did the child recover?" she asked, coolly.

He was slightly taken aback. He realized now he'd hoped she didn't know it all. "Yes," he stammered. "He is much improved. He is not a healthy boy. He suffers from a weakness of the lungs."

She made a noise, but whether it indicated sympathy, disbelief, or merely boredom, he could not tell.

"And Lady Whitcombe?" She sounded as though she were strangling. "How is she?"

"She is well."

"She must be nearly out of mourning, now." Phoebe's eyes were blazing now. "Her husband died only a few months after he killed mine. What a hardship for Lady Whitcombe to be alone with a child. Little wonder she called upon you in her hour of need. But, now that I recollect it, she and Lord Whitcombe had been estranged for quite a long time."

"I believe that was the case." He forced the words out from between clenched teeth. She was playing with him. Like a cat. Making him suffer while he ran this way and that to avoid her. But she would have him in the end. There was no doubt of that. "You would know the London gossip better than I."

"Quite a long time, as I recall. Why, I believe they've kept separate abodes since the days when you were in London. But then, I recall you said you hardly knew Lady Whitcombe."

Oh she was cruel. She wanted to hurt him, and she cared little how much she hurt herself in the process.

They walked along in silence for a moment. He toyed with the idea of embarking on another conversation, but there would be little use. What had happened had happened, and he would have to deal with the consequences.

"How old is this child?" she asked after a long moment of silence. The seams of her gloves were stretching to the bursting point around her fists.

"Almost eight," he said hoarsely.

"Almost eight years," she said, putting her finger to her chin as though she were musing. "Conceived nine months before that. Hm. What were you doing then, eight, nearly nine years ago? Why . . . I believe"—she flung around to face him—"I believe you were engaged to me."

He was run through. Finished. Better put a swift end to it. For both of their sakes. He wanted to reach out to her. He could see she was trembling with rage and pain. She was going through, all over again, what he had hoped to save her from.

"What is it you want to hear me say, Phoebe? That Will is my son? That he was conceived nine years ago at the very time when you and I were engaged? Is that what you want to make me say?"

She opened her mouth to reply, but for a moment no sound came out. "I don't want it to be true," she whispered at last.

"It is."

He had expected her to hate him. He knew that she knew already, so how could her loathing grow stronger? But it had.

She visibly drew herself up, though he could see that she was trembling. Her eyes were wild, dilated, like a woman going mad. He had done this to her.

"You got a respectable woman with child. A lady of quality. Another man's wife. And yet you had every intention of continuing our engagement?"

He stood there, unable to say anything. He'd made his choices long ago.

"You packed her off to some cottage in Bedfordshire on her own. You had no intention of aiding her. Oh, you can make all the noises you like about her being married already, and Whitcombe not giving her a divorce, but you sent her off years ago with every intention of marrying me. Thank God I ended our engagement!"

He'd been a fool. There had been a part of him that believed that long ago Phoebe had loved him. And he'd idiotically thought that that phoenix had risen again during their time together in Cambridge. Now he saw his nascent hope shrivel and die. "Yes," he said dully. "Thank God you ended it."

Twelve

"Nearly two hundred pounds," Phoebe said with satisfaction. "Enough for that dratted millinery bill anyway."

Hillary looked over her shoulder. "Good heavens, you've amassed quite a bit. I do hope you aren't denying yourself things just to save money. There can be such a thing as too much economy."

Not when it meant escaping this place.

She would miss Hillary and her family of course, but there was no helping that. There was absolutely no way she was going to stay in the same town as Jordan more than a moment longer than necessary.

She forced her mind back to the numbers. Otherwise her brain would just keep covering the same conversation again and again. Jordan had a son by Eleanor Whitcombe. Impossible. It was all wrong.

She began toting up another long line of expenses.

"Well, I'll leave you to your clerk's work," Hillary said cheerfully. "Hartfield will be wanting his tea and I must speak with cook before I go upstairs to see my angel." She dropped an affectionate kiss onto Phoebe's brow. "You are doing well, my dear. Everything quite accounted for and every penny squeezed until it squeaks." She grinned. "I'll have you wearing pinchbeck buttons and buying day-old bread next."

Forty, forty-three, fifty-one. It couldn't be possible. Jordan wouldn't have just packed Lady Whitcombe off to live on her own in the country. It wasn't like him at all. Fifty-three, no sixty-three. A child. By Eleanor Whitcombe. She lay down her pencil and pressed her fingers to her eyes.

"Ma'am"—Annie put her head in the doorway, her eyes bright—"there's a young gentleman to see you." She had the audacity to wiggle her eyebrows. "You have ever so many admirers these days."

Phoebe made a low noise in her throat. It was likely only Boxty. He'd left in a huff yesterday, but he could never stay angry for long. Perhaps he was able to see sense now. She closed the account book, trying to formulate the correct way to win him over.

To her surprise, the man who stood up when she entered was a stranger. He was doubtless a student, though he did not wear a gown. "I'm sorry to descend upon you like this, Lady DeVaux," he said, his pale freckled face ducked in embarrassment. "I'm Martin Grenich, a friend of Boxty Fuller's. I mean Lord Fuller's," he corrected himself.

Phoebe then recalled the young man's face from the day they'd gone punting. Boxty, suffering from that common university student malady of being incapable of calling anyone by their proper name, had referred to him as Grinny.

The day she'd met him, the boy had spent most of his time making a fool of himself over Mad Jack's sister. Now though, he seemed gravely serious.

"Hello, Mr. Grenich, may I offer you some tea? You look rather shaken. Is everything all right?"

"I am shaken," he admitted. "I've come for your help."

"Is it—"

"Boxty," he finished. The freckles seemed to stand out in high relief on his nose. "Boxty's gotten himself in a bit of trouble."

"What happened? Where is he?" She felt her own hand tighten at her throat.

Grenich must have realized he'd said things all wrong, because he caught her arm as though he thought she might faint. "He's fine, madam. He's alive," he assured her, fanning her vigorously with a newspaper he grabbed from the table.

She gently detached him and sat down. When he showed no signs of ceasing his flapping, she stood again and took the paper carefully from him. "Where is Boxty?" she asked again, careful to sound less worried than she felt.

"The Granchester jail."

She sat down again heavily. The knot in her stomach bumped, then lay still. He was safe at least. He hadn't driven his carriage off a bridge or set his bed on fire. "Is he all right?" she asked, just to be certain.

Grenich looked at her as though she were lack-witted. "Well," he said cautiously, "he's in jail."

"I mean, is he hurt?"

The young man's shoulders lifted in a kind of shrug. "Not much, I suppose. He's got the devil of a head on him. And a lump from the turn up, but mostly he's just dead anxious."

She wasn't certain exactly what this meant, but

before she could ask, the tea tray arrived and for
several agonizing moments she was obliged to sit
and smile as though there were nothing wrong. At
last they were alone again. "What can I do?" she
said quickly "Tell me how to help him."

Grenich chewed a hangnail for a moment. "See,
if anyone finds out, he'll be sent down. Which would
please Boxty well enough, but his parents would cut
him off without a groat until his majority. Which
would be highly inconvenient for everyone. Very unpleasant. You know how parents are about getting
sent down."

She didn't, but she nodded.

"So I didn't know who to go to except you. I know
Professor DeVaux would help, but he's certain to
feel obliged to tell the master, and then Boxty would
be out for certain."

"I don't think DeVaux would tell," she said, honestly. "Unless Boxty's done something very bad."

Grenich looked at her, leapt up with the paper,
and began fanning her again. "Just larks, ma'am.
Really." A heading in the sporting news caught his
eye, and he unfolded the paper to examine it. "Dash
it all! I had ten pounds on Cooper-Beemish."

"Do you need money?"

He looked up, and folded the paper up again with
a look of guilt. "Money would help." He looked
around him, as though searching for a hint on how
to approach a difficult subject. "But primarily we
need someone . . . respectable to fetch him down."

"Respectable?" She decided that the ten years between herself and Grenich must to him appear a
wide gulf indeed. "You wish for me to go and speak
with the jailer? To bail him out?"

"I never would have asked you if I didn't think that there was another way."

"Just let me get my reticule."

The afternoon sun was valiantly fighting out from behind the morning's fog as they drove down the road to Granchester. It was another of those miserable days that couldn't seem to make up its mind as to whether it would rain or sun and ended up doing a bad job of both. Grenich evidently was so much relieved by her agreeing to accompany him that he felt well enough to stare Annie out of countenance and nearly overturn the carriage in the process.

"How long has Boxty been in jail?" Phoebe asked, trying to draw his attention away from the poor blushing girl.

"Since late last night," he replied, giving Annie a very broad wink.

"Why didn't you come down to me earlier?"

He looked at her with a slightly wounded expression. "Wouldn't have done to call upon you too early." He straightened his cravat and then had to readjust the plunging team. "Lord Fuller was not in the best of form, you understand."

Phoebe was prepared for the worst when she alighted from the carriage, but the jailer seemed a reasonable man, once bribed and flattered to the proper degree.

"Now 'ee ain't a bad genkemun," the jailer granted, rubbing his gristled chin as though he were petting a favorite cat. "Mr. Fuller likely merely suffers from high spirits. Like so many of our young men."

"Lord Fuller," she corrected automatically.

"Is 'ee?"

She realized she'd just doubled whatever fee she'd have to pay. They man's brows rose up in high grizzled arcs in an expression she realized was supposed to denote pleasantness.

"These 'ighborn genkemun 'aven't a sense of propriety when they're in their cups. Is 'ee your brother?"

"No." She thought of explaining, but decided it was pointless. She slid a few more coins across the splintered table. "If Lord Fuller is sober enough, I'd like to see him now."

The man rubbed his nose with his dirty palm for a long time, but at last got up from his chair and indicated with a jerk of his head that she should follow.

The jail was not a big one and the cell was only a few steps down a corridor. The closeness and the smell were unpleasant, but at least there didn't seem to be anyone else presently incarcerated in the two other empty cells. The rooms were small, with the tiniest of windows very high up in the wall. Boxty was in the last one, sitting on a pallet with his head in his hands.

Phoebe stood at the gate until he looked up. His eyes were red and his cravat was undone. He looked so ill that she crouched down so he wouldn't have to get up. "Boxty! Are you all right?"

He flinched at the sound of her voice. "Hullo, Lady DeVaux," he said at last.

"What happened to you?"

"Rode his 'orse up the stairs at the Three Tuns tavern, got in a mill with one of his mates, stole Mr. Wheeler's punt, shot a hole in the bottom of it with a pistol, nearly got himself drowned, fought with his rescuers, and—"

Boxty stopped the jailer's recitation with a baleful look. Then with visible effort he turned his eyes back to Phoebe. "Why are you here, ma'am? This was Grinny's doing. You ain't to know about this."

"Boxty, this is very serious. You were lucky you weren't killed."

His look of contrition was overwhelmed with one of acute nausea.

"You shouldn't have come," he said hoarsely at last.

"Well I have come. And I'm going to get you out of here before someone finds out and you are sent down."

"I don't care if I'm sent down," he said with sudden passion. "You won't marry me, I hate university, I'm an utter disappointment to DeVaux—"

"Don't be ridiculous," Phoebe said briskly. "You're only working yourself into a state. I know it's satisfying. I used to do it myself when Arthur first died. But I assure you, it's most unproductive."

Boxty just slumped further down the wall and sighed with a look of such genuine despondency that she reached toward him through the bars. He did not look up at her gesture.

She turned back up the little hallway and motioned that the jailer should follow her into the main room. "What do I need to do to secure Lord Fuller's release?" she asked calmly.

Grenich, who had been sitting on a small wooden bench along the wall, came up to stand beside her. "There was no real harm done," he said with a hopeful smile. "Boxty will see to it that all the property is paid for." He looked at the jailer with wide eyes. "It won't ever happen again, sir."

"T'ain't up to me," the man replied with a laconic shrug. "I can't just decide who I want to let go."

"Whom do we talk to then?" she asked, struggling to keep her voice polite.

"Mr. Wilkins, the magistrate," he said with a toothsome smile. "But he's out." He pulled a face of false sympathy while he stroked his beard. "Gone out and won't be back until late today or perhaps tomorrow." He shrugged his shoulders and then took out a pouch and began packing tobacco into his pipe. It was obvious he was in no hurry to solve their problems.

The senior combination room was heavy with the scent of smoke, sherry, and the pompous mustiness of age. Jordan liked it. It was soothing. It reminded him that this room, the college, the university, the planet—they would all be here long after he and his petty little problems were long gone.

It was an evening kind of room, but on a misty morning like today, it was perfect if one wanted solitude, but somehow could not stand the silent stillness of one's chambers. The room was empty, as it was too early for most of the fellows. Though they'd be here soon enough, rattling their newspapers and murmuring over the latest gossip.

He heard the door open and recalled that he should probably turn the page in his book to at least preserve the fiction that he was engrossed in reading.

It was too late. Caldwell walked in and looked around. He came over with a look of relief on his face, and then lowered himself into the chair opposite.

"You're up with the larks," he said with a cheerfulness that sounded slightly forced. "Haven't seen you in an age." He cleared his throat and adjusted his position in the chair. "Where have you been off to?"

"Potton," he replied, without looking up.

Undaunted by Jordan's repressive demeanor, Caldwell leaned forward and helped himself to the pot of tea on the table. Apparently they were going to have a coze. "Potton eh? Gone to see the child, I suppose? Nothing amiss, I hope."

"He's recovering." How the blazes did everyone know about Will? Then he reminded himself that there was a time when he'd hardly bothered to keep it a secret. Devil take it, he'd announced his role in the scandal with perverse pride.

"Excellent, excellent." Caldwell took a sip of tea and seemed to consider things for a moment. "And Lady Whitcombe?"

"She's very well."

"Excellent," he said again. "Charming woman. We all went sledding last winter, if you recall. The boy was delighted. I hope to see them both at Cambridge again."

Jordan recalled with a vague sense of surprise that Eleanor and Will had been to Cambridge not so long ago, when he'd convinced her to take the boy to a physician in town. He was surprised Caldwell remembered the event.

"I'm certain they'll be back," he lied. Not while Phoebe was here.

"Have you a mind to go riding? I'm to meet some

men from Granchester in a bit. You look as though you could use it. Your trip appears to have burnt you to the socket." His friend smiled encouragingly. "Come on, it will do you good."

"I must get some work done. I missed an entire week you know."

"Nonsense." Caldwell stood. "It will take your mind off your troubles."

Jordan reluctantly got to his feet and followed Caldwell out into the courtyard. It was drizzling and gray compared to yesterday's bright weather. Had it been only yesterday that he'd walked along the backs with Phoebe? God, how she must despise him.

"Not much of a day for riding," he grumbled to no one in particular.

Caldwell was walking along, his hands locked behind his back, deep in thought. He stopped mid-stride and looked at Jordan. "Perhaps you can give me some advice."

"Certainly," Jordan replied, wondering how his friend ever got the impression that he was qualified in that department.

Caldwell continued on toward the stables, but remained silent. "Well, it's a rather delicate subject," he said at last.

"All problems are, aren't they?"

"There is a woman," he said at last.

Jordan crushed the urge to protest that he was the last person on earth to offer advice on women.

"There is a woman whom I find I have grown particularly fond of," Caldwell continued. He shot Jordan a worried glance then went back to frowning at the ground.

Jordan felt his teeth beginning to clench. Please let it not be Phoebe.

"A widow," Caldwell said with obvious reluctance.

Dear God. First Fuller and now Caldwell? Would every man in Cambridge throw himself at her?

"And I would most like to recommend myself to her attention. But I cannot."

"Why?" He forced out the word.

"Because of you."

Jordan stared at him, stunned. He forced out a laugh that sounded alarmingly bitter. "Really Caldwell, whatever small affection was between the lady and me was forgotten long ago."

"Yes, yes," he said rather too dismissively. "Everyone knows that. Everyone knows the whole of it."

Jordan stumbled over his own feet when they refused to move. "Do they?" He wasn't even sure he himself knew the whole of it.

"Well, if you'd wanted to marry her, you would have done so long ago. I know you are fond of each other, but I cannot believe you love each other. I mean, one only has to look at you when you're together to know neither of you is in love with the other."

Jordan felt the world tilting oddly beneath him. "Indeed," he said, with as much neutrality as he could muster. "And does the lady return your regard?"

"I begin to believe she might, DeVaux. I didn't want to mention it to you, for so many reasons. But it has come to a point where I must."

Jordan could feel fabric of his existence shredding. This was impossible. Phoebe loved Caldwell.

Caldwell did not appear to notice the spectacular

collision of emotions that was happening in front of him. "I know you'll say that we are hardly well acquainted," he continued, "but I assure you my feelings and intentions are entirely honorable." The man unclasped his hands, twisted them, then clasped them behind his back again. After a moment he cleared his throat. "I know she's very much attached to you, because of your past. And of course there is the matter of the child."

"Yes," he said, feeling rather ill.

Caldwell seemed to be feeling as agitated as he himself. "I mean, dash it all, could you bear to see me raising your child?"

The earth seemed to stop its revolutions. "What the devil are you talking about Caldwell?"

Caldwell stopped as well and stared at him for a moment. "Lady Whitcombe," he replied, bemused.

The world gave a lurch and now seemed to be spinning too fast. "Eleanor Whitcombe? You're in love with Eleanor Whitcombe?"

Caldwell looked slightly wounded. "Is it so remarkable? I know . . . her past . . ."

Eleanor. Not Phoebe. How stupid he had been. Eleanor, a widow. Eleanor, who was not in love with him. He felt the tension fall away from him. "Not in the least. Not at all. She's a lovely woman. And if she returns your regard, you have my blessing." Everyone had his blessing. Everyone in the whole world.

They'd reached the stable now, but Caldwell hung back from the yard filled with hostlers and grooms. "But don't you see?" he said in a low, urgent voice. "The world will think it terribly scandalous. We all knew that she could not marry you because Lord

Whitcombe would not grant her a divorce. Since his death, though, everyone has been waiting for you to right that situation."

"Oh," he said stupidly. He and Eleanor had half-heartedly discussed marriage, but she had insisted that her neighbors were quite willing to pretend that Whitcombe had fathered the child, and that there was no need for him to make such a sacrifice. He saw now why she'd had no enthusiasm for the idea. How blind he'd been in his selfishness.

"Hallo!" came a booming voice from around the corner of the stables. "I thought I should find you here. You're a lazy sort, Caldwell. We were supposed to be out and about hours ago." Three men, all roly-poly caricatures of country squires, rode up. "Dash it all," said the oldest, flinging himself off his mount, "you university men. All thought and no action."

Jordan took these to be their companions for the day and bowed his greeting. He wished he could find an excuse not to go. He needed some time alone to digest the latest information. Of course the fact that Caldwell and Eleanor had some budding romance hardly changed the fact that Phoebe still wished him to the devil. But now, even being back in the same miserable position he had been in this morning seemed like a relief.

And, his mind ran on, if Eleanor and Will were taken care of, there was no reason he could not explain the whole bumblebroth to Phoebe. She would be upset, and rightly so, at his secrecy, but perhaps, someday, she could understand. He looked around at the men, who were laughing their chesty laughs and slapping their mounts with wide, beefy hands.

The last thing he desired was a day out with the sporting set. But it looked as though solitude was going to be impossible.

"I thank you," Caldwell murmured, under the hubbub of introductions. "You've set my mind much at ease."

Feeling much more cheerful than he had in ages, Jordan grinned. "And you mine. In fact, I was thinking of going back to Potton in another day or two. Perhaps you'd like to accompany me?"

Thirteen

The magistrate's house was only two streets over on the side of a leafy square, but the small, round butler who answered the door squinted down his pug nose and informed Phoebe primly that His Worship Mr. Wilkins was out and was not expected back for several hours. Loath to drive back into Cambridge without their friend, Phoebe, Annie, and Grenich sat down to coffee at a reasonably respectable-looking little coffeehouse and sat looking glumly at each other.

"Once the magistrate comes home, I'm sure we won't have any trouble," Phoebe said again, stirring a little vortex in her cooling cup.

"Wish I knew someone studying law," Grenich grumbled. He'd said this before as well, but his companions merely nodded mutely. "Can't be fair to just lock a man up."

Phoebe considered reminding the boy that Boxty had indeed destroyed several people's property, but they'd covered that ground already, so she held her tongue. "It's a rather nice day," she said instead. "The mistiness of the morning is quite burnt off. We could walk around the town for a bit."

Neither her escort nor her maid looked enthusiastic about the prospect, but the three of them duly got up and went to pace the length of the square a few times. Another hopeful call at the magistrate's house continued to find him not at home and with no projected time of return. Disheartened, they made their way back to the jail.

"Shall we go back and ask again?" Grenich asked. He obviously considered her the leader of their little rescue effort.

"I can't see that it will do much good," she said irritably. "But I don't know what else to do. I hope he will let us see Boxty again, and we'll just have to explain to him that we've done everything we can for the time being, and that we'll leave a letter with Mr. Wilkins and come back this evening."

Grenich's boyish look of helplessness reminded her how much older she was. "Annie," she said, "please remain behind with the carriage. Grenich, come with me and we'll see what we can do."

She marched inside, trailed by Grenich, who, with the delicate sensibility of youth, was rapidly growing despondent.

He had good cause to be. The jailer informed them that Lord Fuller had become quite obstreperous, had hurled invectives offensive to the jailer's tender ears, and was now barred from seeing any visitors. Even the few coins she and Grenich could scrape together after the mad extravagance of the coffee were not enough to soften his heart.

"You'll 'ave to see the magistrate," the man repeated. He pocketed the money, and then went back to picking his teeth with the point of his dinner knife.

Grenich shot him a plaintive look. "Just for a moment, sir? To cheer him up a bit?"

The jailer looked him up and down. "M'mutton's getting cold."

They walked outside in silence, each mulling the problem at hand. If Boxty had to spend another night in jail, he would be missed. He would be sent down for certain. And while ultimately Phoebe wanted him to follow his dreams out of Cambridge, she didn't want to see him leave in disgrace. Jordan would be so disappointed.

She looked up with some surprise to see that there was a man standing next to the carriage talking to Annie. But rather than looking embarrassed as she had with Grenich, the girl looked as though the sun had just risen. Something in his bearing gave her a strange sensation in the pit of her stomach. It was Jordan.

He turned around, his smile without warmth. "Lady DeVaux, Mr. Grenich," he said, bowing.

"How pleasant to see you in Granchester," she said quickly, hoping Annie had had the sense not to mention their mission. "I had just stopped here to ask after Mr. Jenkins's wife. She's my mantua maker, and she's been ill of late. Oh, I see you've ridden. I would have asked you to walk with me around the square, but I'm certain you're in a hurry." She pretended to tighten the ribbons of her bonnet and then turned to Grenich. "Mr. Grenich, thank you for your kindness in driving us here. It was so fortuitous that we should happen upon you."

She found that the three of them were staring at her with varying expressions of alarm, helplessness, and blank assessment.

"Come, Annie," she said, shooting her maid a look of warning. "Shall we walk down to Mrs. Jenkins's shop?"

She was several steps away before Jordan said anything. "You didn't happen to see Boxty when you were in the jail, asking after Mr. Jenkins's wife?" he asked dryly.

"Boxty?" she repeated, her mind racing for some new story to tell him.

"Yes." He leaned his elbow on the shiny lacquered surface of Mr. Grenich's curricle and examined her with an attitude of utter ease. "I went out riding this morning with several friends of friends. One of whom happens to be Mr. Wilkins, the magistrate. He just happened to mention that there had been a bit of trouble last night and that Lord Fuller is in the Granchester jail."

There was no point in pretending. "The jailer won't let us see him," she announced. "And Boxty doesn't want to see you, anyway. He'll be devastated to know that you heard of this bumblebroth. It was merely high spirits; there was no real harm done. A violent hangover is the worst of it. Mr. Grenich and I will take care of everything."

Jordan's eyes narrowed slightly. She had the strange impression that he was judging her. That he was seeing something new in her that he was not in the least bit certain he approved of. Slowly he reached into his waistcoat pocket and withdrew a piece of paper.

"May I offer you this then?" he said, coldly. "It is Boxty's release. Mr. Wilkins was kind enough to give it to me." He put the paper in her nerveless hand, bowed to her, and with a nod to Annie and Mr.

Grenich, he turned to go. She could see the tension in his jaw, but he merely wished them a chilly good day and mounted his horse.

Phoebe thrust the paper into Grenich's hands and turned him toward where the jailer had come to the doorway to watch the little drama unfolding.

"Wait," said Grenich, "this notes that the fine was paid in full." He looked toward Jordan. "Sir, I cannot allow it. On Boxty's behalf, I must insist that I call upon you later and repay what he owes."

Jordan surveyed them all with his impassive gaze. "As you wish," he said serenely.

Without even realizing that she'd meant to do so, Phoebe found that her legs had carried her to Jordan's stirrup. "Walk with me," she commanded in a tense voice. "I must speak with you." For a moment she thought he would refuse her, and then, with a faint sigh of annoyance he swung down from his horse.

She managed to stay silent for long enough for them to get out of earshot. "Any anger you feel toward Boxty you should direct toward me," she said, looking at him to be certain he was listening. She wished she hadn't. The direct gaze of his dark eyes made her go all trembly.

"And why is that?"

"He's merely in a fit of the sullens because he's been thwarted too many times. You know he's a good young man, and you know he behaves with a great deal more sense than most of your other students."

"Precisely why I'm angry with him now. He's not the most clever of my students, but to see him wasting what talent he has on starts like this . . ."

"You judge him more harshly than anyone else because you care for him more than anyone else."

His dark brows pulled together but he did not deny this. "And how is all of this your fault? Now, Phoebe, if you think he went off on a juvenile bender because you wouldn't marry him, you're more vain than I thought."

She meant to keep her face a blank but he must have seen the expression of hurt. "There, now, I shouldn't have said that. He likely did, to tell you the truth. And he wouldn't be the first, unfortunately. Lord knows I did when you threw me over," he muttered under his breath.

She ignored the hot blush that suddenly rushed to her cheeks. He had had Lady Whitcombe to console him. "There were many reasons he mentioned," she stammered. "Not the least of which is the fact that he's not happy here. He stays here because of you, Jordan. And that's the only reason. I'm certain the other fellows would have been glad to have sent him down by now. Boxty himself wishes for it, and I cannot believe that his parents would not forgive him. You are unwilling to let him go."

A muscle jerked in his cheek, but Jordan said nothing.

"Boxty cares for you as though you were his father. He would do anything to please you, no matter how he hated it." She took his sleeve. "And I know you like him better than students who are twenty times as clever. But you cannot bear to let him go. To let him become something that he really wants to be."

"Don't preach a sermon to me, Phoebe," he said irritably. "Next you'll be trying to convince me that

Boxty should be congratulated for his pranks and that it is entirely unreasonable for me to have tried to instill in him what little knowledge his mind can hold."

She realized she must have wounded him more than she had meant to. "Everyone knows how much you have done for Boxty. Not the least of whom is Boxty himself." He had not yet thrown her hand off his sleeve, so she tucked her fingers within his elbow. "Don't you know that is why he was so anxious that you never find out about this incident? He cares more for your opinion than anybody's. He is miserable thinking that you will be disappointed with him."

"I am," he said, immovable.

She looked at him, feeling for a humiliating moment as though she might, inexplicably, burst into tears. "Do you ever forgive anyone once they've disappointed you? Is it utterly impossible for you to believe that someone who admires you and would do anything to have your good opinion might live so much in fear of living up to your impossibly high standards that they might make the very kind of mistake they were hoping to avoid?"

He stared down at her for a moment, as though she were an unexpected stain on his cravat. "I hardly call riding his horse up to the attic of the Three Tuns tavern, boxing the watch, and subsequently shooting a hole in the bottom of a stolen punt an innocent mistake."

"He's angry. Angry with me for refusing to marry him and, more to the point, angry with you for judging him so much more harshly than any of your other students."

"Enough," he said sharply. And then, perhaps realizing how cruel it had sounded, he said it more gently. "Enough. I will not reprimand Boxty for this incident. He need never know I know of it."

Her smile of gratitude was frozen by his look of icy indifference.

"I would ask, however, that were a situation like this to arise again, you come to me or to Professor Caldwell for assistance. You should not be in the position of rescuing young fools from their follies and certainly not when it involves going to places like this on your own." Jordan made a jerky gesture toward the jail.

"Mr. Grenich came with me," she protested. The nervousness she felt at seeing him was being replaced with a kind of tense irritation. "Besides, I'm a widow. I am invisible to the world."

He took her by the shoulders and turned her roughly toward him. He looked as though he wished to read her another harsh lecture, but to her shock he kissed her hard on the mouth.

He pulled away before she had the chance to even respond. "I wish that you were," he growled. Then he turned on his heel and went over to mount his horse.

Fourteen

Phoebe's confused mind boiled all the way home, and by the time Grenich had deposited her and Annie on the tidy steps of the Hartfields' house, she felt as though any rational thought had quite evaporated away.

The last time she'd seen Jordan, he'd admitted to fathering a child by Lady Whitcombe during the very time of their own engagement. She'd hated him. She'd loathed him. He'd betrayed her with a saber cut to her trust and there was nothing that would make the memory of their brief time together anything but bitter.

It didn't make sense. When she thought of those days, even with the jaundiced eye of hindsight, she still believed he had loved her. Could he truly have looked at her with that expression of adoration, even professed his love for her, while all the while having an affair with Lady Whitcombe? It made no sense. She knew him. She had once felt as though she knew his soul.

And even if it was all true, why had he not married Lady Whitcombe? As Boxty said, perhaps they were waiting for her to complete a decent cycle of mourning before they married. As though they hadn't flaunted every other propriety.

It was too horrid to contemplate.

And despite it all, she still loved him. It was only because she was tired, confused, and angry that she felt the hot prickling behind her eyes, but there was no way to stop it. She could feel them coming, a mad riot of tears fighting their way out, and she hurried up the stairs, desperate to reach the safety of her room.

"Good heavens, Phoebe, what has happened to you?" Hillary stepped out onto the landing as she barreled past.

"Nothing, nothing. I just . . . the wind has blown something into my eye, and I must wash it out." She scrubbed at her face with her handkerchief.

"Oh, my dear, how awful for you. Come into my room, and I will help you. I know how painful that can be." She took Phoebe by the hand and led her up to her own frilly chamber. "There now, here's the basin. Is that better? Oh my, but your eyes are red. Both of them. Is it so windy out? I was thinking I should go and see Mrs. Lane, but I can't abide going out in the wind. I really would prefer rain if it comes to a choice. The wind always musses my hair and it seems like the umbrella is always turning inside out. That is, if it is raining too. Which is the most unpleasant of combinations. But of course, to-day has turned out rather better than expected. Except for the wind."

By this time Phoebe had managed to control herself. She washed her face and dried it on the towel Hillary offered. "There. I am recovered. Thank you."

"Are you certain?" Hillary looked closely at her. "You look so pale. Perhaps it is only that your hair is blown about. Here"—she unpinned Phoebe's curls and began brushing them out—"you had best start all over again."

Hillary's kind ministrations somehow brought her even closer to the breaking point. How dare anyone be kind to her when she was so miserable? "How is the baby?" she asked, hoping to distract the woman.

Hillary beamed. "Ever so much better. You know I would never have thought to visit Mrs. Lane if he was not. My little lambkins. He was so very cross. But now the toothache is gone and the colic is gone, and he's just the prettiest angel that ever walked the earth."

She wondered what William Whitcombe looked like. Did he have Jordan's dark eyes? His curls? Did he have that way of smiling where the left side curled up first?

"Not that angels are generally thought to walk the earth," Hillary was saying, the brush suspended in her hand. "And not that my darling has yet to actually walk either."

"Where is he?" she asked.

"Sleeping. I wanted him to take his nap early so that he can stay up late for the celebration."

"What celebration?" Oh dear God, please don't let it be—

"Jordan came home yesterday," she said, oblivious to Phoebe's wince. "So we're having a dinner. *En famille,* you understand. But we will have turtle soup. I was determined. I am quite cross with Jordan for having run off with no notice at all."

"I . . . I suppose he had business to take care of,"

she said, unsure what Hillary knew. She certainly had no desire to protect Jordan. It was Hillary's feelings she was concerned for. It would kill her to find out what a wicked, heartless man her brother was.

"Yes, well I suppose we couldn't help it that the child was ill." Hillary shook her head in disgust. "Though the boy has gotten an inflammation of the lungs every spring since he was born. And that silly woman thinks he is dying every single time."

Phoebe stared at her, shocked. "You know?" she whispered, unable to make the words come out in more than a rasp. "You know about Lady Whitcombe?"

Hillary looked slightly taken aback. "Oh dear, you didn't? Oh, I should not have said anything! I thought you knew!"

"I did," she assured her friend, stammering through the renewed wave of nausea. "I just thought *you* didn't."

Jordan's sister raised her shoulders in a gesture of one accepting fate. "Of course I was not happy to hear of it. But one grows used to these things, I suppose. He told me years ago. And the way he carried on, you'd have thought he expected me never to speak to him again. But of course, he's Jordan, and one can't very well stop loving him."

Phoebe said nothing.

"He supports her you know. And goes to see her every time that boy has the sniffles. He has since the first. Whitcombe never sent her a shilling. Though of course they were estranged for years before she even met Jordan. Whitcombe wouldn't grant her a divorce though." She began carefully pinning Phoebe's heavy blond locks back into place. "My brother has set her up quite tidily."

Phoebe stared blankly at her reflection in the mirror. Her traitorous mind was going back, back to the time when she had been engaged to Jordan. They hadn't told anyone, thank heaven. Like the children they were, they'd hoped to wait until Jordan's prospects were better before they approached their parents. But that hadn't made it less real. Or at least it hadn't to Phoebe. Jordan, apparently, had been gallivanting about the town the entire time. She felt sick, even after all these years.

Hillary smoothed the hair on the crown of Phoebe's head. "I hope we haven't shocked you. I really thought Arthur must have told you. We don't talk about it often of course, but it is something that Jordan has been most honorable about. I mean, of course, it shouldn't have happened in the first place, but we would be naïve to think such things did not happen, however regrettably, and once it had, he behaved most properly."

"Arthur knew too?" Was she the only one kept in ignorance? How peculiar that her husband had not told her. It would seem as though he would have jumped at the chance to show her that her former love was not the paragon she'd set him up to be. Perhaps Arthur had thought to protect her.

"Oh yes, I'm quite certain that he did," Hillary was continuing. "In fact, I recall that Jordan wrote him about it. You'd hardly think he would have wanted to advertise the fact to anyone, but I do recall that he wrote to Arthur in particular. They'd always been so close, you know." She put the brush back on the dressing table and gave Phoebe a thoughtful look in the mirror. "At least when they were young."

"Indeed," she said, not knowing what else to say. She thought she was going to choke. Her stubborn mind did not want to take it in. It didn't make sense. Why, if everyone knew, and Jordan was not particularly ashamed of it, had he denied, just weeks ago, that he had known Lady Whitcombe back in London? Was it merely to spare her? Had he thought that since Arthur had not tattled on him, no one else would?

Hillary's moment of pensive thought had passed, and she was fluttering again. "Oh dear, you still look quite pale. Do you have the headache? Perhaps you should go lie down for a little while." She began opening and closing all the drawers in her table. "I know I have a tisane in here that is just the thing. Oh dear, I can't recall where I put it. Well, here, take my lavender pillow instead and have a bit of a lie down. Then you'll be fresh for the dinner party. I would be so despondent if you were to miss it. We are having turtle soup you know."

She looked so hopeful that Phoebe could do nothing but take the proffered pillow, thank her and slowly make her way upstairs. Only four in the afternoon. Impossible. So much had happened. And she'd made a muddle of it all. It seemed like ages ago that she'd refused Boxty's offer of marriage.

And then to discover that she was the only one who had not known of Jordan's child. It was embarrassing, really. Even Arthur had known.

In the middle of her little sitting room was that hateful box from the solicitors. There was nothing in it now but the sheaves of bills and dunning notices, but of course she would always remember the humiliation it contained. Arthur, Jordan, was there no man in her life who had been true to her?

It was far too much to think about. And impossible to stop thinking about.

She sat through dinner, chewing, swallowing, smiling, and nodding like a clockwork windup toy. For all she knew, she'd eaten the napkin and drunk a glass of gravy. The conversation was jovial and ordinary, just like the other evenings when Jordan had come to dinner. Only those had been merely awkward. This was excruciating. Now they sat in the parlor while Hillary entertained them on the pianoforte, accompanied by Hartfield's snores.

Phoebe and Jordan sat on the settee, the silence between them louder than either of the Hartfields. He'd avoided looking at her all evening. He'd spoken commonplaces, but he'd never once looked her in the face. Angry? Ashamed? She tried to remember that she didn't care.

"Where's that nephew of mine?" Jordan asked, preempting another concerto. He rubbed his hands on his trouser legs. "Couldn't leave without the grand finale. He must have grown a foot since I saw him last. He's probably off at Eton by now."

Hillary giggled and rang for the nursemaid. "Don't be ridiculous, Jordan. Though that bothersome tooth did come in at last. And I do think the dear's eyes might be turning the slightest bit hazel. Is that possible? I've heard they do change."

Hillary's son was brought in with due ceremony and deposited in his uncle's arms.

Phoebe felt as though her heart had exploded,

embedding painful shrapnel into her rib cage. Jordan held the baby so naturally. Had he held William that way when he was born? Or had he not even been there for the child's birth? She tried to calculate where Jordan had been when William would have been born. She herself had been married to Arthur by then. Married seven months. She hadn't wanted a long engagement. Dear God, had her wedding anniversary come and gone without her noticing? She felt a flush of guilt.

Despite Hillary's claims that the baby had recovered from his previous attack of the crochets, the creature fussed and wiggled in Jordan's arms. "Little eel," he said fondly, as the baby continued to try to escape. "Forgotten who your uncle is, eh?" He laughed without humor as the child made loud inarticulate noises of protest and reached out to Phoebe for rescue.

"Do you want Cousin Phoebe?" Hillary asked in her talking-to-baby voice. "Go to Cousin Phoebe."

Jordan obediently went to pass the child into her arms. The man was too close, too real. She could smell the scent of his skin and the starch in his linen, and she could see the tiny lines just beginning to form at the corners of his eyes. She willed strength back into her knees.

"I've been thinking about what you said," he said quietly.

Her eyes flew to his, and she realized he was looking at her for the first time. "What?"

"About Boxty. About how he would be happier if he left school."

She hadn't wanted to talk about Lady Whitcombe or the child. She hadn't wanted to talk to him at all. But in a way she'd been stupidly hoping for an explanation from him. Something. Something to reassure her that he had genuinely cared for her. Back then. When it had mattered.

"Did you ask him?" She put the baby over her shoulder and pretended to be absorbed in soothing him. Hillary went back to the pianoforte to play a lullaby.

"No. Not yet. I was just thinking about it. I discussed it with John Caldwell. You will be gratified to hear that he agreed with you entirely." He looked away, cleared his throat, and then caught her gaze again. "I just wanted you to know that I took your suggestion seriously." Something in those sad dark eyes gave her a tightness in her stomach, as though she were looking over the edge of a precipice.

"Thank you," she managed to stammer. She put more space between them. "I'm glad." Poor Boxty. He struggled so much when he really shouldn't have to. She wondered for a moment what it could have been like if she had accepted his suit. They could have gone back to London and lived an ordinary life. It would have been better than what she had had with Arthur. Better than most people's lives, perhaps.

"I will speak to him tonight," Jordan went on, "after the course at the observatory."

Mention of the observatory brought back a flood of memories she'd rather not recall. "What are you lecturing on tonight?" she asked, with an admirable attempt at normal conversation.

"Tonight we will discuss orbits." His smile was stiff, but she knew he was trying just as hard as she was.

The weight of the baby was comforting on her shoulder. The creature was shoving his tiny fingers into her hair, pulling at the curls Hillary had so carefully dressed, but she found she didn't really mind. "And what does one need to know about orbits?"

"Well, we begin with Newton's revision of Kepler's third law, work through calculation of the earth circling the sun and the moon round the earth, and then talk a bit more about the orbit of comets." He seemed to realize what he said and stopped. "Why are we even pretending, Phoebe? I know how you feel about me, and I don't blame you in the least."

She looked at him in surprise. His eyes were intently upon her, and his expression made her throat go dry. There was a terrible buzzing in her head. She didn't want to think about this anymore. It was too confusing. Too awful. But he was standing in front of her, still waiting for her to speak.

"I should have told you the truth long ago," he said quietly when she remained unresponsive.

"Yes," she said quietly, looking him full in the face. "But the truth is that Lady Whitcombe's son isn't yours. He's Arthur's."

Fifteen

There was a terrible silence. It took a moment for Jordan to realize that it was caused not so much by the shock of Phoebe's statement as by the fact that his sister had finished playing.

"Oh dear," Hillary exclaimed, "Hartfield has fallen asleep. That dreadful man, he always does that. I suppose music does soothe the savage beast. Though port does help, as well, I think. There now"—she bustled over to where he and Phoebe stood in charged silence—"how is my love behaving? Oh naughty! You've pulled down Cousin Phoebe's hair. He does so love to pull things apart. Here, hand him to me." She took the child in her arms.

Jordan stared at Phoebe, but she seemed completely engrossed in putting the cups back onto the tea tray. His efforts to catch her attention and demand that she explain her shocking pronouncement were ignored.

"Perhaps you would like to walk down to the observatory with me," he said at last. At the last minute, he realized he had to extend the invitation to the whole family. "All of you, of course. The night is fine; the moon is quite full."

Hillary was about to demure, but he managed to

convey with a look that this was something she should accept.

"Yes," his sister said enthusiastically. "What a lovely night this is. Wouldn't that be charming, Phoebe?" She stepped over to ring for the baby's nursemaid.

Phoebe flicked a glance at him, then gave a jerky nod.

"Dear me, I shall have to wake up Hartfield. He would love to accompany us as well, I'm sure. And even if he doesn't, he must, because Jordan is going to have to give his lecture and I must admit I have no desire to listen to a whole lecture on astronomy just to wait for him to escort us home again." Hillary smiled her best matchmaker's smile. "Now, get our coats, and I'll just give Hartfield a shake."

She herded them out of the drawing room and into the street. After a few moments of awkwardness, too short for explanations and too long for comfort, Hillary and Hartfield joined them and they started off. It was a lovely night. Too much moon of course, but lovely in the conventional sense.

The tension between himself and Phoebe was like a live, writhing thing, threatening at any moment to break the bonds of social order and run amok.

He could see her smiling tensely, her pace measured and careful as they walked toward the observatory. He allowed his sister and her husband to walk on ahead of them so that he and Phoebe could continue their interrupted conversation. He could feel it hanging in the air, crackling like a fuse.

"I'm right, aren't I?"

Her mouth was tight, white around the edges. He

didn't know what she wanted to hear, but at the moment he thought he would say or do anything to take that look of misery off her face. "No," he stammered. "Will is my child. I don't know how you got such a silly—"

"I've been a fool," she interrupted, "but I'm not one any longer. Arthur was never faithful to me. I knew that, I suppose, though I never wanted to examine it closely."

He wanted to take her in his arms. He wanted to hold her while she suffered. But he forced his hands to remain at his sides and did not move.

"I found letters. Among Arthur's things. Letters from his lovers." He saw her shoulders rise and fall in the dark. "I suppose I should not have been surprised. After all, we'd lived separate lives for many years. But still, it was"—her voice trailed off as she tried to think of the right word—"wounding," she ended at last.

He did take her hand now, but she did not appear to notice. For the first time in weeks, a dart of hope shot through him.

"There were no letters from Lady Whitcombe, but that makes little difference," she went on. "I knew your character, and I knew Arthur's. What is remarkable is that the whole world swallowed this tissue of lies knowing it too."

He didn't know what to say, so he continued walking along in silence. In front of him, he could hear Hillary and Hartfield talking in low voices.

Phoebe's face was pale in the moonlight. "What I don't understand," she said, "is why you pretended the child was yours."

It had been a long time since he'd even considered that decision. Much less questioned it. He gave up at last and decided on the truth. "Because Arthur was married to you."

She stumbled and his arm went around her waist. He let her go instantly, but the terrible familiarity of her body was painful.

"But I saw you and her . . . kissing . . ."

"Lady Whitcombe came to me when Arthur turned her off," he said quietly. "She was furious. Her husband wasn't about to support someone else's brat and Arthur said he wouldn't see her taken care of. She wanted to publish the letters she had from him."

"And you stopped her." Her voice was hoarse.

"I believe what you saw was my putting her in a coach to Bedfordshire. I only hoped to help her and to save Arthur and our family from the embarrassment of seeing the letters published. When I said I hardly knew Lady Whitcombe, I told the truth. At the time, she was only a woman who was so wounded and frightened that she desperately needed my help.

The story, once started, was a strange relief to tell. "I had no intention of claiming her child then. But shortly afterward you broke our engagement and married my cousin."

He shrugged. "I did not think you deserved the humiliation of knowing your husband's foibles. And what did it matter if the world thought the child mine? I had no one to answer to. I pay for the child's upkeep and Eleanor and Will live quite happily in the cottage near Potton."

He could feel her hand trembling. "Why did everyone assume that I needed to be taken care of?"

she demanded. "Why was everything kept from me? Do you know how stupid that makes me feel? As though everyone in the *beau monde* knew of Arthur's perfidy and your nobility except me?"

"Very few people knew," he said quietly. "These little scandals happen all the time."

She was silent for a long time. "I would have liked to have known the truth."

"Would it have changed anything? You were already wed to him."

Her hand had somehow become disengaged from his. He wanted to grope for it again in the dark, but he knew he could not.

"No," she answered at last. "It wouldn't have changed anything."

They were at the observatory. He could see the students making their way toward it in twos and threes. He tried to recall the topic of tonight's lecture. This was hardly the time to be delivering lectures on anything, much less astronomy.

He didn't want to leave her. Now that the secret was out there seemed to be so much more to say.

"Did . . ." She looked up at him with an expression of hesitancy. "Did Arthur have any other children?"

He realized now that he'd entertained foolish hopes that she would understand that he had done all this for her. It had been the young man's notion of a heroic martyr jilted and still very much in love. But still, even now, he'd somehow hoped she would know he'd done it to spare her pain. But all she thought of was Arthur. "I don't know," he said quietly. "I don't think so."

"And Lady Whitcombe?" Her voice was small. "Is she all right? Is she happy?"

"Yes," he assured her. "She is far better off without Arthur or her husband." He turned to go, but her hand on his sleeve stopped him.

"Is that why Lord Whitcombe shot my husband? Because he found out?"

He nearly lied. It would have been so much easier. But there had been so many lies. "No. It was over a mistress. Once again Arthur had cuckolded Whitcombe."

She seemed to think about this for a moment. "You have to go now," she said at last. "You'll be late for your lecture."

"I'm sorry, Phoebe."

"I needed to know. I'm sorry I didn't know earlier, but I needed to know."

He looked down at her for a moment. In the dark her face was all shadows and luminous whiteness. She looked so fragile. He and Arthur had both disappointed her.

He tried to remind himself that she'd made her choices long before he made his. He tried to recall that she had broken his heart first. That she had chosen to end what was between them. Still, a part of him wished that he had had the courage to fight for her. And had not burnt so many bridges behind him when he'd gone.

Sixteen

"You're out of your mind, Phoebe," Hillary said for the fourth time. "It's such a long journey. Would not a letter do?"

Phoebe finished cording up her traveling case and sat back on her heels. "No. And you know as well as I do that the trip will do me good. Lady Whitcombe was kind enough to allow me to visit, and I would like to see this child for myself."

Hillary's mouth tightened. "I'm sorry Arthur was not a better husband to you. If I had known that he let Jordan take the blame for his mistakes for all those years . . ."

Phoebe got to her feet and dusted off her skirts. "That was Jordan's decision." She looked out the window to see if the traveling coach had been brought around. Jordan and Arthur had been the best of friends as well as cousins. Inseparable. She'd known she'd wounded him when she jilted him for Arthur.

How angry he must have been with both of them. She almost flinched as she recalled the day she'd told Jordan she would not marry him. How had she had the strength? She didn't know how he'd heard about her subsequent engagement to Arthur. By that point they were not on speaking terms.

And yet he'd claimed Arthur's child to spare his cousin the scandal of having his letters published and to save her the humiliation of knowing her new husband had betrayed her. He was the noble hero and she the faithless jade. It was a lowering feeling indeed.

"Promise me it won't be a long trip," Hillary said. She pulled out a handkerchief and began twisting it. You've become part of our family now. Baby will cry every night if you aren't there to pay pat-a-cake with him."

"A sennight at most. I would not dream of descending upon Lady Whitcombe for longer."

"And how kind of Lord Fuller to drive you there. He's been quite devoted to you of late." She raised her brows in a manner that could only be called insinuating.

Phoebe smiled. "Don't you dare start getting hopes in that direction," she assured her friend. "I assure you that I have no intention of marrying again. And were I to even consider doing so, it would not be to someone so many years my junior, however kind he might be."

Hillary raised a shoulder in a kind of shrug. "I only want to see you happy. And I cannot see that going to visit Arthur's child is going to resolve anything. As Jordan said, it will only stir up trouble and upset Lady Whitcombe. 'Tis better to let things go on as they were."

Phoebe pretended to check the knot of the cord. Was she being selfish? Was it wrong of her to wish to see this child? It was not merely idle curiosity. She needed to be certain the family had everything they needed.

She'd already written to her solicitor to request that some of her widow's portion be sent to the boy. It would slow her own escape from Cambridge, but it was what Arthur would have wanted. No, that wasn't right. Arthur hadn't cared about the creature's existence. It was what Jordan would have wanted.

Annie came up to announce Lord Fuller's arrival and Phoebe followed Hillary down to find Boxty trying in vain to compose his lanky form on the settee.

"Lady DeVaux, Mrs. Hartfield," he said, unfolding himself and rising, "you'll never guess what has happened. Just what would please me most. At least it would have pleased me most if it wasn't such a dashed inconvenience to you."

"What are you talking about, Lord Fuller," Hillary asked.

"Letter from my father," he replied, flapping a piece of paper. "I'm commanded to go home instantly. Seems Professor DeVaux came through for me after all. Wrote m' father and suggested I go on the grand tour straight off instead of waiting until I graduate. I never thought they'd agree, being that they'd been so dead set on my getting a university education before I went, but Professor DeVaux explained that I would learn much more there, and that one of his fellow fellows—ha ha, a fellow fellow! Isn't that a laugh! Professor Hillyard is planning on going abroad with Joxer and Grinny. So m' parents said I could go as well."

"That's wonderful news," Phoebe agreed. How

very kind of Jordan to arrange that so diplomatically. Perhaps he had listened to her after all.

Boxty's brows drew together. "Not for you," he said. "Must go back to London immediately. Commanded, you understand."

"Of course. I'm delighted for you."

"But you"—he looked anxious—"you want to go back to London too. I would feel very badly if I were to leave Cambridge and you had to stay here."

She wondered briefly if he intended to renew his suit, but he looked merely concerned. "I'm all right," she assured him. Yes, part of her still wanted to go back to London. She could escape this place and all the uncomfortable emotions associated with it. But when she tried to picture her life, once again, without Jordan, her mind quickly veered away in alarm.

"Don't be ridiculous," she said instead. "I never intended that you should wait for me to go back. You must certainly do as your parents ask. Oh, I'm so happy for you, Boxty."

He smiled. "You don't have to postpone your trip to Potton if you do not wish to. When I went to tell Professor DeVaux about the news and explained that I was only sorry that I would inconvenience your plans, he said he would escort you."

Phoebe's heart began pounding very loudly in her ears. "How kind," she said faintly. She'd wanted to be alone. Or if not that, alone in her thoughts while Boxty rambled. She needed time to think, and it would be so much harder if the object of her thoughts was with her. "I'm certain Professor DeVaux has other obligations. My trip can wait until a more convenient time."

She could hire postillions, of course, but the thought of the expense made her cringe. She'd saved so carefully in the past few months. This journey was likely only going to bring heartache anyway. Perhaps she should not go at all.

She'd barely made the decision when the butler announced Jordan himself. He walked in looking calm, just as though everything were perfectly ordinary. Just as though the tension between them was not vibrating the air with an almost audible crackle. Phoebe felt as though her legs were about to give out beneath her. Too many events had happened over the last few days. She didn't know how she wanted to feel and her emotions had taken the bit between the teeth and were running wild.

"Are you ready to go?" he asked, just as though he'd planned to escort her all along. "Caldwell is coming with us. I didn't think you'd mind. He wished to come in, of course, but I said we didn't have the time. Shall we go then?"

Hillary began fussing at him to take off his coat and to bring Professor Caldwell in for some tea before they left but he politely declined.

"You can't go with me," Phoebe burst out at last. "You must have other things to do."

He smiled then. "It is hardly to China, Phoebe. I will take you there and come back by Sunday evening. You may stay with Eleanor as long as you like. When you are ready to come home, someone will fetch you. Caldwell perhaps. He needs a good reason to go."

It was reasonable of course, but it was strange enough going for a visit to see her husband's ex-mistress and his child. It would be a thousand times more humiliating to do so under Jordan's scrutiny.

"Come on," he said, taking her arm. He flashed a sudden grin. "Things could hardly get *more* awkward between us."

The journey was not nearly as horrible as she had imagined it would be. Caldwell sat in unusual silence, but Jordan kept up a stream of easy remarks, avoiding explosive topics with the same skill with which he drove the team.

"There is no need to be nervous," Jordan said calmly to both of them as they turned up the lane toward Lady Whitcombe's modest cottage.

Phoebe noticed she was twisting her gloves in her lap and forced her hands to still. "I'm not nervous," she lied.

"Eleanor is hardly a monster. And I'm certain she is feeling just as uneasy."

Eleanor. For some reason it stung her that Jordan was on first-name terms with the woman. He'd been her protector in the literal sense, if not the sexual sense, for the last nine years. And one only had to look at his quiet, eager face to see that he loved her.

Arthur had loved her too. He'd cast her off just like he eventually did every woman, but he had loved her. Phoebe pushed back the feelings of jealousy and fear and turned her attention toward the modest cottage at the end of the road.

A woman came down the steps just as the carriage rolled to a stop. Her hair was a fiery chestnut, spun with golds and reds like an autumn wood. Her dress was simple but suited her tall, elegant figure and classical features. Beside her, Phoebe felt pale and wilted.

"Lady DeVaux," the woman said, extending her hand as they climbed down from the carriage, "how very kind of you to visit. I'm delighted that you have come."

Phoebe shook her hand in a daze then stood aside while the woman greeted Jordan and Caldwell. "Nothing would do but for her to come see you," Jordan said with a smile. "She refused to believe that I had taken care of anything suitably."

The woman looked up at him with adoring eyes. "You have done everything, DeVaux. You have been angelic in your goodness." She looked back at Phoebe. "All my happiness in the world is possible because of him," she said passionately.

Phoebe stretched her mouth into a smile. So this was the woman Arthur loved. The woman Jordan had sacrificed his reputation for. The notorious Eleanor Whitcombe. Phoebe's own life seemed a barren existence made up of card games and shopping trips. She had been so ignorant.

"Won't you come in and see Will?" Lady Whitcombe asked. "He's much better. You'll be so pleased, DeVaux. He asks for you every day and was in raptures to hear that you were back again so soon."

The woman flicked an uncertain glance toward Caldwell, but then turned toward the house. In the parlor, there was a pale, thin boy just coming away from the window seat, where he had evidently been on the lookout for them. He flung himself into Jordan's arms.

"Will, my boy! How could you have grown in two weeks? You're looking fit as a fiddle. Keeping your mother in torments?"

"I've been very good," the boy protested, injured. "And I haven't been sickly at all."

"Excellent. I'm very glad to hear it. You know Professor Caldwell of course, but there is someone else I'd like you to meet."

"Lady DeVaux," the boy filled in. "The wife of my father."

Phoebe jerked in shock to hear it put so calmly.

"I thought it best that he should know from the beginning," his mother said quietly.

"Hello, William," Phoebe said, unsure of proper etiquette.

Will performed a perfect bow, shook her hand, and then continued to look at her with grave curiosity. "You are a widow now," he said at last.

"Yes. Lord DeVaux died over a year ago."

He frowned a little. "I never saw him. He didn't want to hear about me. So I don't much care that he's dead. But I'm sorry for you."

"Thank you," she said at last, not knowing what else to say.

They stared at each other in silence for a moment.

"Why did you want to see me?" he asked, tucking his hands behind his back and regarding her anxiously. "Are you going to take me away from my Mama?"

She sat down without being asked, her legs no longer strong enough to hold her. "No, no of course not. I just wanted to see you. I wanted to be certain that you and your mama had everything you needed."

Will's chin went up. "Professor Lord DeVaux takes care of us," he said defiantly. "He is a professor at Cambridge."

"I know," she said. "And he is a very noble man." There was a tight knot in her throat that made it difficult to speak.

The boy looked so much like Arthur. His hair was dark and curling, his chin determined to be square, but those eyes were not the same. Arthur had always been laughing, anything serious made him quickly bored and then annoyed. This boy's dark eyes were somber, as though he had never laughed. But the resemblance was there, too, striking. She could not help but stare.

"Perhaps Lady DeVaux would like to see your garden," Lady Whitcombe suggested. "I'll have the tea things set out on the lawn, and we will all take our tea there when you are finished."

Phoebe saw Jordan go to the bellpull and instruct the servants just as though he lived here. How strange that they had all been living a life she knew nothing about. She felt oddly left out.

Arthur could have told her. She would have been hurt, yes, but not shocked. Or he could have supported the boy without telling her. But Arthur hadn't even wanted to acknowledge him.

She dutifully followed Will out into the garden. It was a muddy little plot, but they both pretended great interest in the progress of the beans and lettuce.

"I suppose I should try to be more sad that my father is dead," William said at last. "But I don't really feel it."

Phoebe wondered if Arthur had even known that the child was a son. "You don't have to feel sad," she said. "You just need to take care of your mother and stay well. I know she worries about you a great deal."

He nodded, then bent down to capably secure a fallen vine to a stake. "Do you have children?" he asked.

"No."

His brows rose in an expression that reminded her of Arthur. "No? How peculiar. Everyone I know has children. I am the only one I know that is only one of one. I don't play with the other children much. I'm usually not well enough. And Mama likes me to be near her."

Phoebe began extracting some stray weeds lurking under the turnips. "If you are ever curious to know more about your papa, I hope you will ask me."

When he did not answer, she wondered if it had been the wrong thing to say. What did she know of children? Particularly ones with such grave faces and intent expressions.

"I used to wonder," he admitted at last. "I used to wish that he would come and take me to London and give me presents and a horse." He made a face as though to imply that that was a long time ago when he was a naïve child. "But once I heard Mama say that my father was as bad as her husband, and so then I didn't want to know him anymore." He examined the leaves of the turnips with an expert eye. "Do you think that sons always turn out like their fathers?"

"No," she said immediately, "I don't. You have many traits of Arthur; you are handsome and clever and capable of great things. Your father did not use his talents. But you can use yours. And you have two very important people to guide you, your mother and Professor DeVaux."

William appeared to digest this for a long moment. "I will do my best," he said at last, in his most serious tone.

He looked up and saw his mother crossing the lawn. "Ah, here is Mother. Tea must be ready. I hope we haven't gotten too dirty." He brushed off his knees and then, with a gesture of careful politeness, offered her his arm. He looked at the table where his mother, Caldwell, and Jordan had set up tea outside and were waiting for them. "What a strange little party we make," he said, smiling the first faint smile she had seen from him.

"Yes," she agreed. "A strange little party indeed."

Seventeen

Jordan drove to the little cottage in Potton several times during the week Phoebe spent there. It wasn't as though he didn't have dozens of other things claiming his attention. But somehow he found himself on the Bedford road nearly every day.

Eleanor would have teased him about it if she didn't know very well that he would retaliate with the comment that as often as not he arrived to find that John Caldwell had beaten him there.

Jordan didn't really wish to analyze why he was so anxious to go; there were many other things he should be doing, and there were times when he found it almost physically painful to be in Phoebe's presence, making pleasantries, smiling, when all the time he was wondering what was going on behind those green eyes.

She and Will had taken to each other like long-lost siblings. It was gratifying to see them working together in the garden, or riding out with Will mounted on the little Welsh pony Phoebe had badgered him into buying. Jordan hadn't realized how much the two needed each other. Will was lonely, isolated by his frequent illnesses and his overprotec-

tive Mama, and Phoebe . . . Well it was obvious now
that Phoebe was pining for someone to love.

"I know she tries not to spoil him," Eleanor said
with a sigh as they sat on the lawn watching Caldwell,
Will, and Phoebe playing a spirited game of croquet.
"And she always defers to my judgment, but I cannot
help but worry that all this excitement is not a little
too much for him."

"Nonsense," he replied. "It's done him a world
of good. I should have been spending more time
here myself. It's time the boy had more to do. You
can't wrap him in cotton wool forever."

"You are right, of course." She smiled. "John says
the same thing. He insists I coddle the boy too
much. But I will not have you thinking that you have
not done enough. Lord knows what would have become of us if you had not stepped in." She poured
another cup of tea and added a bit of sugar. "I've
enjoyed Phoebe's company this week. It is a strange
comfort to befriend her after all these years. Fate
has an ironic sense of humor."

She turned to watch Phoebe as she and Will fell
into a vociferous and comical argument over the le-
gality of running alongside one's croquet ball and
shouting encouragement that it roll in the correct
direction.

"Will she remarry, do you think? It is obvious that
she adores children."

Jordan felt a tightness in his chest. He'd thought
about that more lately. Her mourning period was
over. She knew the truth about Arthur and seemed
to accept the fact that her husband was not the saint
she had previously thought him to be. Did she feel
the same pull that he did? Was it folly to even con-

sider the idea that they might, nine years later, consider trying again?

"I don't know," he said truthfully. She had told Boxty once, not so long ago, that she would not. Did she feel differently now? Evidently Boxty had hoped she had, since he had proposed to her himself. "I know she would like to go back to London. I'm certain at some point she'll take herself off, and we'll find that she's married to some Town Dandy like Arthur with a brood of children for her to mother." He didn't mean to sound bitter, so he tacked a loud laugh on just to be certain Eleanor didn't get the wrong idea.

She frowned. "I hardly think he will be like Arthur."

He opened her sunshade for her and handed it to her. "Why do you say that? She worshipped him."

The woman pressed her lips together and looked out across the lawn. "Will, don't take off your coat. I know it feels warm, but you know how susceptible you are to chills." She shot her son a warning look to be certain he complied, then turned back to Jordan. "I think it was you who worshipped Arthur," she said quietly at last.

"What are you talking about?" An uncomfortable wash of annoyance made him snap his teacup back into its saucer and sit back, arms crossed. "Arthur was a bounder as you and I well know."

Eleanor gave him a thin smile. "That never stopped you from loving him."

"Nor you," he shot back.

"Nor Phoebe, despite it all." She watched with a look that was almost sad as Caldwell and Phoebe stood together gravely discussing strategy, while Will cheerfully called attention to the fact that he was winning. Eleanor sighed. "Arthur was a charming man. He had the ability to seem both powerful and vulnerable. When he made mistakes he was always contrite, and when he was in love he was so very, very in love." Her smile now was far away. "We all let him get away with anything."

When she looked back at Jordan, he noted the weary look around her eyes, the way her mouth turned down at the corners. She was likely the same age as Phoebe, but her life had been more difficult.

"You let him get away with anything," she said, returning to the topic Jordan hoped she had forgotten. "I know you and Arthur were close in boyhood, but you never lost your admiration for him. You never really saw his faults. Arthur used to talk about it. Brag about it, really. He knew he could run up gaming debts in Town and that you'd pay them. He knew that if his parents got upset, you would pacify them. You were his squire, his faithful companion." Her sad mouth tightened. "But he took terrible advantage of you."

Jordan waved a languid hand. "Not in the least. We were both bucks about Town then. Game for any madness. Just the foolishness of young men. If I did him any favors, he would have done the same for me."

"Were you never angry that he married Phoebe?" Eleanor asked in a calm voice. Her expression was penetrating. "I know of course that you were engaged to her. It wasn't common knowledge, but Arthur told me. Back when"—she hesitated—"back when we were together."

This conversation was not going in a direction he

found comfortable. He had known Eleanor for a long time, they were friends, but they had never felt the need to examine each other's hearts. "That was years ago," he said with a shrug. "Eons. And Phoebe was but eighteen. Young ladies of that age often change their minds about engagements."

"He wanted to have what you had," Lady Whitcombe said quietly. She carefully sipped her tea and then looked at him. "He always wanted to have what you had. And you appeared to have everything." He made a noise of dismissal, but she pressed on. "Don't you know that the world considered you the more charming? The more handsome? And though Arthur had the title, everyone was already speculating how long it would take for him to run though his inheritance."

"Nonsense. We were like brothers."

"Like Cain and Abel," she said, with a laugh that held no humor. "Arthur did love you, but he was jealous of you as well. He was jealous of anyone whom he thought had more than he did. He was capable of great love, but it was always tinged with his love of self."

"I'm afraid you might be considered a rather biased judge of his character," he said. He did not want to hear this. Arthur was dead. The ambivalence of his feelings for his cousin, his strange, convoluted feelings for his cousin's wife; they were best not disturbed. And certainly not to be discussed over tea on the lawn.

"I am biased," she admitted. "But you know it is true. There were good things about him, but he hurt a great many people."

"Yes," he said shortly. He knew Eleanor was not

the only broken heart Arthur had left in his wake. There were many rumors of his passionate attachments and tempestuous partings.

Eleanor looked out across the lawn. "Arthur wanted Phoebe. He told me. Perhaps to hurt me, I don't know. His passion for me had cooled, and I was mad with jealousy. Arthur hated the fact that Phoebe had never even considered him, but had given herself heart and soul to you."

The memory of those days came back to him, glossed with the sickly sweetness of lost love. They hadn't really been the way he remembered them. They couldn't have been as magical as his memory pretended. He was only recalling what he wished to recall.

"Eleanor, those days are long gone. I see little point in dragging them to light again. You are happy here with Will, Phoebe is learning to accept her life in Cambridge, and things are at last peaceful. Why must we analyze the character and motivation of my reprobate cousin? Let the past lie."

"Did you know he forced himself upon her?"

His heart stopped in his chest. "What?" He hadn't heard right. The buzzing in his head and the painful rip of shock down his limbs had distracted him. "I'm not sure what you mean."

"Why else do you think she married him, Jordan? Because she suddenly decided she loved him?" Eleanor fairly spat out the words. "You were so busy being noble and letting her go that you didn't figure it out. And then before you could, you'd leapt in to play the martyr by pretending that William was your child to save Arthur's reputation. And he let you do it." She closed her eyes, but not before Jordan could see the hatred in them.

"I don't blame you," she continued, calmer. "I didn't know either at the time. No one did." She opened her eyes and looked at him. "I never would have let you claim Will if I had known."

Good God, it couldn't be true. His mind refused to take it in. He didn't know what he felt. He was going to bellow and break up the furniture, he was going to cast up his accounts, he was going to race across the lawn and shake Phoebe and demand to hear that it wasn't true.

Eleanor's low, insistent voice kept coming. "I see how much she loves you. I see that she'd never stopped loving you. We've talked a good deal in the past week."

"Did she tell you what happened?" he demanded.

"No." She forced a smile and waved at Will, who was hooting in triumph and running in circles on the lawn. "But she slipped in something she said, and I pressed her. The conversation had turned to children, and she mentioned that she had always wanted them, but that Arthur had hardly touched her once they were married." Eleanor's expression was tight and angry. "There was the unspoken implication that before their marriage it had been a different matter. I thought of course, that they'd merely, well, you know what I'm trying to say . . . Become amorous prematurely? But that was not the case."

"Would Phoebe lie about something like that?" he wondered aloud, almost hoping that she would. If she had not, the truth was too horrible to contemplate.

Eleanor's fierce eyes pinioned him. "Would she?"

He knew it was true. And if he had been less self-absorbed he could have seen it as well. Phoebe had loved him. Her affection had not suddenly wavered in favor of his handsome cousin. But he had been too hurt to consider the reason behind her sudden decision to marry Arthur. And then, with the mad carelessness of thwarted love, he had shocked the town by claiming Eleanor's child and then sequestered himself away in the safe, mild haven of Cambridge.

He leapt to his feet, with the half-cocked notion of going to Phoebe and demanding that she tell him what had happened. Eleanor's cool hand on his arm restrained him. "Jordan, you look wild. Don't go to her now; you will frighten her. I should have said nothing. She would not have wanted me to say anything. I doubt she knows that I know it all. I have only fit the pieces together recently. I only thought you should know that it really was you that she loved." She gave him a rueful look. "I let my tongue run away with me. You know I have bitter memories of Arthur DeVaux, and I should not have added this smirch to his character."

Rage was boiling hot within him. "Why didn't she tell me?" he exclaimed. "Did she think I would discard her? Did she think I would take Arthur's side over hers? That I wouldn't have done anything to help her and protect her?"

Eleanor was looking at him with eyes that now held alarm. As though he'd changed into a violent, frightening beast like his cousin. "I don't know, Jordan," she whispered at last. "I don't know."

Eighteen

Phoebe knew he was angry. The straightness of his spine and the rigid way he held the reins spelled it out easily enough. For a while she pretended to ignore it, hoping that he would be jollied out of it by her stories of Will's latest pranks and her own ludicrously foiled attempt to cheat at croquet.

She lapsed into silence and stared up at the stars from the open carriage. Annie was dozing, her chin sinking down to her chest, her usual prattle stilled. Phoebe wished Caldwell had come with them and had not ridden back on horseback on his own. Then she wouldn't have to keep up this ridiculous one-sided conversation and could simply enjoy the gauzy beauty of the summer evening.

"I thought I would try to come down again on Tuesday next week. Eleanor is picking strawberries to make preserves and I said I would help. I know you don't lecture—"

"I can't go."

"Oh. All right."

She lapsed into silence again and looked up at the sky. It was a clear night, thick with stars. The sky was so bright with them that she could see the silhouettes of the trees on the horizon and could make out the starlight through every slender branch.

"I hope you don't mind my accepting Eleanor's invitation for dinner. I hadn't thought about driving back after dark. But she seemed so anxious to have us a bit longer, and I know she enjoys playing whist. She has had too little company for so long that it seems unkind to deny her small pleasures."

"She has you."

She turned to him but his expression was impossible to read in the dark. "Are you angry with me for being her friend? I meant in no way to criticize you. Heaven knows that you have been the best friend to her anyone could be. Why I can't—"

"I asked you once why you married Arthur," he said suddenly.

"Arthur? Whatever—"

He leaned toward her, his voice low, but intense. "You made up some silly story about seeing me with Eleanor."

His tone was full of such suppressed fury that for a moment she was afraid of him. This wasn't the gentle, slightly wounded question he had asked her that day on the Cam. This was an accusation. "It hardly matters now, Jordan."

"Arthur compromised you, and you had to marry him."

His words hung in the clear night air like the tone of a bell ringing long after the clapper has struck the metal. Phoebe felt a sick tightness in the pit of her stomach. She never should have said anything to Eleanor. She'd thought the woman hadn't noticed her slip, but of course she had. And, knowing

Arthur as she had, she'd drawn exactly the correct conclusions.

"I made the decision that seemed the only option at the time."

"The only option!" he echoed incredulously, pulling up the horses sharply. He didn't seem to care or notice that Annie had awoken and was looking around in confusion. "We were engaged to be married. How could you possibly believe that you didn't have other options?"

She cringed at the harsh note in his voice. "Don't make a scene, Jordan," she said, shooting a glance at Annie, who was squinting in bewilderment at the suddenly raised voices. "We'll discuss this later."

"No. We'll discuss this now. Annie, get out of the carriage."

"Sir!" the maid exclaimed, fully awake now. "Please, don't drive off and leave me on the road in the dark!"

"Annie, I will not—Fine. Phoebe, get out of the carriage. We're going to sort this out right now."

He got down out of the carriage and gestured that the groom riding behind should hold the horses. He did not even look behind him to see if Phoebe had managed to climb down to follow him.

Once they were out of earshot of the servants, he turned on her, "Tell me how you could possibly have thought that I would not understand and support you if you told me that something like that had happened."

She shuddered at the coldness in his voice, but steeled herself. She wasn't certain she'd made the right choice. Not then, not now. But it had been hers to make and she had made it. "I liked Arthur," she began. "I liked him because you liked him. You idolized him. And at first he seemed to support our romance. But then, he started to tease me about it. Silly things at first, telling me that you were flirting with other women, that I would have to keep a sharp eye out once we were married. Bantering, really. But with a cruelness about it.

"I was young and very much in love. I believed that everyone must love you as I did, and the idea made me jealous. It was ridiculous, I know, but he made me doubt you. I did see you with Eleanor. I saw you kiss her and put her in a traveling carriage. I know now that you were only helping her. That you'd secured money for her and made traveling arrangements so that she could have Arthur's baby far from London."

He said nothing but waited for her to go on.

She sighed. There was little point now in keeping anything back. "And then, once doubt had been seeded, Arthur began to flirt with me. At first, just nothing, pretending that he was disappointed you had won my affection, things like that. It was all done with such an air of fun that I never thought to complain to you about it. After all, he could do no wrong in your eyes."

She could tell he didn't understand. He had no idea how it had been in those days. And she didn't blame him. The story was coming out all wrong. It sounded silly; petty stories of jealousy and mistrust. How could Arthur have held such influence over them both?

She thought of Arthur as she'd seen him last with his laughing eyes and his innocent smile. Yes, even when she knew his character exactly, she still was captivated by him. He could be kind and generous, but he could be demanding and cruel as well. It was a dangerous combination and even now she could not explain it. When he wanted something he would stop at nothing to have it, but it was the horrible sweet selfishness of a baby.

"Tell me what happened," Jordan said with a quiet calm that was somehow even more frightening than his former anger.

She started to resist, but stopped herself. Jordan deserved to know. He should have known long ago.

"Do you recall the night you went to your mother's house? She had fallen ill again—I don't recall now what it was. You and I had planned to go to Vauxhall, but you told me that you could not go after all. I was disappointed, so when Arthur offered to take me along with his party, I accepted. I should not have gone. It was loud and vulgar and Arthur had obviously drunk too much. He walked with me down one of the darker paths and tried to kiss me.

"I was angry, but he was more insistent than he should have been and then his friends came upon us. By then my gown was torn in the most humiliating of ways, and I felt like the worst thing in the whole world had befallen me. In retrospect, I was a widgeon. Much worse could have befallen me. Regardless, there were quite a number of people there, enough to convince me that my reputation was utterly ruined. When he came to see my father the next day to propose, I accepted."

A light wind had sprung up and she was conscious of her dress flapping around her ankles. Jordan, in contrast, was absolutely still. She didn't know what she had expected him to say, but he didn't say it. How stupid to have admitted it all. The past was better left there. After all, there was nothing to be done about it now and Arthur was dead.

She stood waiting in the silence, acutely aware of the macadam pressing into the thin soles of her slippers and the ceaseless screech of the crickets in the dark fields that lined the road.

"You didn't come to me," he said at last.

"Would you have believed me?" she asked, surprised at how angry her own voice sounded. "Would you have believed that your perfect cousin was capable of such villainy? You were like brothers. Would you have believed that he wanted me just to prove that he was better?"

She could not see his eyes but his voice was cold. "You play the victim so well."

"You don't even believe me now."

"You never took the chance to find out."

She was furious now, blind with it. "I was trying to protect you. Don't you know how I suffered? I loved you, but I had to marry the very person who kept me from you. I didn't want you to have to suffer the same loss. I didn't want you to know what a selfish person your cousin was."

His steps crunched closer on the gravel. "Protect me." He said the words as though he wanted to spit them out. "You took any choice from me. You can say all you want that you hurt me to ultimately save me from pain, but you decided my future without even consulting me. Without any trust that I could make a good decision and that I would act rightly by you."

She was silent, too many angry thoughts in her head to be able to express any of them coherently.

"We thought we were in love with each other, but we weren't," he went on. "People in love solve their problems together. I loved you, Phoebe, but you didn't love me. Oh, of course you thought you did. And it's so easy to say now that you cared. But you didn't even trust me."

She felt as though someone had punched her in the stomach. All the air went out of her and there was only a sick feeling of emptiness left behind. "No," she said weakly. "That's not true."

"You were so angry with me about William," he went on relentlessly. "Angry that I had allowed my life to be ruined by taking on Arthur's mistake. Don't you see that you did the same?"

"I didn't have a choice, Jordan."

She could see him shaking his head in the dark. "You did. You had many choices. And one choice you made was to take any part in the decision away from me. You may have thought you were trying to protect me, protect Arthur, whatever, but you took it all on yourself, and decided that you knew best for everyone."

She was so furious she thought for a moment that she would attack him, pull his hair, pummel his chest. Didn't he care how much she'd been through? That she'd consoled herself only with the thought that she'd done the right thing? She thought she'd freed Jordan from an engagement he didn't truly want and had protected him from knowing his cousin's true character.

Then the anger went out of her in a rush and there was only a feeling of great weariness. "You only care how this affected you, don't you? You're only angry that you were left out."

He said nothing for a long time, then, as though he were weary, too, he turned back to the carriage. "Come on. It's late."

She followed him obediently, but mounted the carriage on the other side so that Annie was forced to make room for her and sit bodkin. Phoebe saw her maid and the groom exchange a glance of misgiving, but after that everyone assiduously ignored each other as the carriage bounced along in the dark.

What was the point of arguing over what had happened years ago? Yes, Arthur had been wrong and it was terrible what he had done, but there was little point in blaming him now. His selfishness had brought him to his end anyway. What she felt now, strangely, was guilt.

Eleanor and Jordan, and therefore, perhaps, the whole world knew she had not loved Arthur. She'd married him, but it had been a sham. They would never believe that she had grown fond of him, in her own way. Never of course in that knee-trembling way that Jordan affected her, but fond nonetheless. And that she had genuinely mourned him when he died. No, Eleanor and Jordan thought her a liar and a hypocrite as well.

All those years thinking she'd done the right thing . . .

Cambridge seemed very light after the darkness of the countryside. Phoebe was relieved the ordeal was nearly over. There were plenty of carriages carrying various laughing parties to their evening's amusements, and it made the tense silence of the carriage all the more noticeable.

"Thank you for driving us home, Jordan," she said as they drew up to the house. To her horror her voice came out squeaky from lack of use. "I'm sure Hillary would be devastated if you didn't come in."

"Some other time," he said curtly.

"Perhaps you'd prefer to simply slow down, and we can jump out?"

He looked at her, and for a moment she thought he might laugh at her tart tone, but he said nothing.

He halted the horses and let the groom assist them down. From the pavement, Jordan looked very high up, and very stern.

For a moment she felt a flash of anger. She had been the injured party, long ago, when she'd decided she must marry Arthur. Didn't Jordan understand the heartbreak she had gone through? No, instead of feeling sympathy, he thought only of himself. "Good night, Jordan," she said coldly.

To her annoyance, he didn't even bother returning her greeting, but merely urged the horses down the street into the night.

Nineteen

Jordan heaved a sigh as he walked the remaining steps up the hill and sat down on the flat rock just off center from its crest. He had plenty to do, God knew, but as usual these days, he was having trouble concentrating. Only here, on the dark edge of town, could he lie in the grass under the quiet serenity of the stars and find some peace.

For a full month he'd been livid. Door-bangingly, childishly, livid. It was ridiculous, he knew. He should feel sympathy for Phoebe, jump to her defense. After all, she'd been forced into marriage with Arthur. But for some reason all he could feel was rage. He was angry with Arthur for his selfishness, at Phoebe for not telling him, and mostly angry with himself. He'd been a blind fool, and he knew it.

Perspective, he reminded himself. This had all happened a long time ago, and there was nothing to be done about it now. He squinted up at the stars, which stood out in bright patches behind the clouds. He'd been to the observatory earlier that night, but he'd found it nothing but frustrating. He needed perspective there too. He needed to step back and look at the whole sky. So he'd gone to the hill.

He didn't know how long he'd been there, mull-

ing things over for the thousandth time, when he
saw a silhouette coming toward him. For the briefest
moment, he found he'd been hoping it was Phoebe.
He had no idea what he would have said to her. But
he still felt an itch of annoyance that it was only
Caldwell.

"What are you doing here?" Caldwell asked,
though he didn't sound very surprised.

"What are *you* doing here?" Jordan echoed, sitting up. "It must be past three."

His friend flung his hat onto the grass and then
flopped down beside it. "Taught my course at the
observatory tonight," he said, punctuating the statement with an enormous yawn. "Went and lay in bed
for a while, but I couldn't sleep. I tried so hard that
I was getting angry, so I decided to go for a walk
instead."

Jordan smiled for what felt like the first time in
weeks. He'd done the same many times. "Best view
of the sky is from here."

Caldwell made a noise of assent and sat down.

They watched the dark film of clouds slowly cover
Gemini. "Do you ever wish you could look up at the
sky and just see stars like everyone else?" Jordan
asked, breaking the long companionable silence.

"I suppose." Caldwell yawned again. "Though
now, I can't imagine what that would be like. I look
up, I see constellations. It's more complex than
when I was a child, but still familiar. They're like
furniture. They're just there."

"You don't feel frustrated?"

Caldwell raised himself up on one elbow and
looked at him. "Frustrated? Why?"

"Because there's so much we don't know. Because there's so much to be done."

His friend fell back on his back with a groan. "You with the fire in you. Don't you see that as a beautiful thing? We shall always have employment." He laughed and then sobered. "Would you rather study something about which everything is known? Would you rather scrutinize Homer for the thousandth time, hoping to find a new way to think about it? We are explorers, DeVaux. Perhaps we won't know everything that there is to know when we die, but we will have been part of the discovery."

Jordan felt as though he'd stepped away from the telescope and was looking at the sky with his naked eye. Perspective. It was all a matter of how you saw it. "You are right," he said with a rueful laugh. "I do spend too much of my energy straining against the lead."

"You always have," Caldwell said cheerfully. He loosened his cravat and put his hands behind his head.

Jordan looked back at the sky, still musing. Had he made things harder than they needed to be? In his attempt to do things right, had he failed to see all the options?

Caldwell held his fist out at arm's length and made a rough calculation of several angles between the stars. "Like Boxty Fuller," he said at last, still squinting at the heavens. "Devil take it, I should have brought the little repeating circle. I'd have liked to take a more accurate look at the distance between Procyon and Mars."

"What of Boxty?"

"You wanted to make him into something he

wasn't. Turn him into a scholar when he never was meant to be one. Can't turn lead into gold, you know." He paused. "I've seen you do it with Will too—wanting what you think is best for him but never asking what he wants."

Jordan sighed. The cloud had wandered on, and Gemini was bright in the sky again. "Wouldn't it be grand to have an observatory on a mountain above the clouds, where the view was never obscured? Like the one Lenneau has in Switzerland? Damned cold of course, but you'd be cuddled right up to those beauties." He smiled up at the sky.

"I was wrong about Boxty," Jordan said at last, returning to the conversation. "But he's in Italy now. Merry as a grig, finally on the grand tour. Swears he's never going to read another book. And I do believe it." He thought of the change in tone in Boxty's recent letters. He did sound happy. Happier than he'd been at Cambridge, certainly. Jordan felt the familiar pinch of guilt. He'd thought he was doing the right thing, and once again, he'd forced unhappiness on people.

"Always betting on the longshot, you are," Caldwell said with a laugh. "You defended him more times than any other student. You are more stubborn in doing what you think is right than any man I ever met. Like with your pretty widow."

"Lady DeVaux?" he asked, though he knew of course which lecture was coming next.

"Yes, yes the famous Lady DeVaux everyone speaks of. The Lady DeVaux who made the scene in the dining room and who has been seen in your company on numerous occasions over the summer."

Jordan could see the flash of his friend's teeth in the darkness. "I'm certain you recall her."

There wasn't an hour that went by when he didn't. Even just sitting here, he wondered what she was doing now. She'd have closed the curtains to the little upstairs room and blown out the candle. He pictured her asleep, her pale hair down around her shoulders and her face serene. It had been so long since he'd seen her. "I do recall her," he said dryly.

"*That* liason you balked at for some reason," Caldwell continued. "Don't know why, and I don't really care to. But even a fool could see that you were in love with each other. From the very start. There've been any number of bets laid on how soon you'll get yourself leg-shackled. But you've resisted. Lost ten pounds when you hadn't popped it by Easter."

"The lady had something to say in the matter as well, as I recollect," he said. "Besides, has no one in Cambridge anything better to do than gawk at a widow and a professor beating the dead horse of their long forgotten romance?"

"Good heavens, you should have been a poet," Caldwell said with sarcasm. "Well, it matters little to me, and I shan't pry into your affairs. I only care that you haven't been out for a drink with me in weeks, you're a bear to talk to, and I know for a fact that you haven't written a word on that treatise of yours."

"All true statements."

"You need to make a change, DeVaux."

"A new sense of perspective," he echoed, grimly. He got slowly to his feet and brushed ineffectually at the grass stains on his breeches. "It's late. I've grown maudlin and you've grown wise. A sad state of affairs indeed. Will you walk back to the college with me?"

"I will not. I'd better lie here mulling over how to solve your problems, character flaws, and other deficiencies until I am ready to sleep."

Jordan laughed at him. "You shall be a long time at it." He turned and followed the path back down the hill. In the starlight, the pebbles winked back at him under his feet. It really was a lovely night, far too fine for brooding.

He'd put her out of his mind. Out of his mind completely. It would be like those days, if there ever had been any, where he had been so absorbed in his work that the memory of her could not penetrate the fortress of his intellect.

Perversely, his mind went back to the time when he'd first come here, reeling from her rejection and subsequent unexpected marriage to his cousin. She could have spared him that. If she'd only told him what had happened, her true feelings, he would have married her instantly.

He tried to picture it, but couldn't. Too much had happened. They were too different now. Both changed by their experiences, for better or worse. No, it was pointless now to speculate how things could have been.

A night's restless sleep did nothing to restore him. And worse, another less intelligent being seemed to have possessed his body, for he found himself, long before the acceptable calling time, rapping impatiently upon Hillary's door.

To his surprise, it was Phoebe herself who opened

it. For a moment, they stared at each other, with almost laughable expressions of alarm.

"Well," said Phoebe, at last, "I'd better tell Hillary that you've come."

"I don't want to see Hillary. I need to see you."

She gave him a cool look. "So you see me."

"May I come in?"

She seemed slightly flustered, but she moved to let him in the doorway. "Hillary is feeding the baby. I'll just send someone for her."

He took her arm. "No, please. I want to talk to you." He sounded far more desperate than he'd meant to, but he realized, in a moment of clarity, that he *was* desperate.

She was staring down at his hand on her arm, so he removed it. She still looked undecided, but at last led him into the sitting room. As she sat down, she gestured to a seat some distance from her but he found that he could do nothing but pace.

"I hope you are well," he began explosively at last.

"Yes, quite."

"I have not seen you in some time." Good God, what was he thinking? He never should have come.

"No," she agreed calmly. Then, "I hope you have not avoided the Hartfields on my account. Poor Hillary has been despondent."

"Daresay she never noticed." He shrugged. He sat down then, not in the chair across from the fire, but beside her on the settee. "I have been avoiding you. I should not have, but I was very"—he searched for the words—"upset by our last conversation. I wish I had known the circumstances of your marriage to Arthur. I wish—"

"Jordan, there is little point—"

"But there is time now," he interrupted. "Time to rectify everything. There is no impediment now."

"Jordan—"

"Marry me."

She stared at him.

He took her hands and felt his own shaking. "Marry me now and things will be just as they should have been. There is nothing stopping us."

He swallowed, waiting for her response. But none came. The clock on the mantel ticked on and on and still she said nothing. Her expression was drawing tighter and tighter as though she were in pain. He released her hands, wondering if he had pressed them too hard in his ardor, but she did not look relieved. "I cannot," she said in a low voice at last.

Cannot. Would not. Was it possible that the tension building in the last months, the constant draw he felt toward her had all been in his own mind? "Why?" he asked, his voice almost a whisper.

She gave a harsh laugh. "You can't just bound in here after not speaking to me for a month and ask me to marry you. Not after the conversation we had." She stood up and shook her head. "Impossible. I cannot think straight and you cannot be thinking either. There has been too much time, too much gone wrong for us to even contemplate going back to where we started."

"We can—" he began. Strangely, he'd walked in the door not being certain this was what he wanted, and now that she'd refused him, he was more certain than ever that it was the only thing that would ever be right.

"No," she cut him off. "We can't." She drew herself up. "Besides, I'm going to London."

"London?" he echoed stupidly.

"Yes, I'm free of you. I've saved enough and earned enough to pay back my debt to you. Hillary has the account books; she can go over everything with you. I was going to write you today, to tell you, but I am leaving this very afternoon."

"Phoebe—"

"I've taken a little house in Cheapside. Annie will go with me, and I shall hire a companion as well, just as soon as I find someone suitable."

"Why are you running away from me?"

She looked at him. For the first time, he felt as though she were hiding nothing. There was the raw truth on the other side of those eyes. Pain and truth, but no defenses. "I have to do this. I know it seems ridiculous to you, but it is very important to me." She watched her own hands twist in her lap then looked up again. "I have always based my decisions on what was right. What other people told me was right. I married Arthur because my father told me I had no choice. I tolerated Arthur's wild ways because it is what wives do. I came to Cambridge because you said that I must."

She smiled, and it was neither bitter nor happy, but instead was small, almost hopeful. "I am going to do something, for the first time in my life, because I want to. Because *I* think it is right. No one else. I have the chance, as a widow of no consequence, to at last be free of society, free of family, free of everything but my own inclination."

The childish part of him wanted to howl and stamp his feet. He wanted to shout that he loved her and he wanted her and it wasn't fair. But in the face of such a trusting, open expression, he could only smile sadly back at her.

"Of course, Phoebe. I'm sorry I played a role in your tyranny. You know it was not my intention."

To his surprise, she placed her hands in his. Her gentle touch brought on an ache he could hardly bear, but he could not bring himself to pull away.

"Of course not," she said with a smile. "We both made wildly bad decisions in the past. But they were always made with the best intentions."

They had been. And somehow she now felt it was best to cut her losses. It had somehow come to a choice of her marrying him, or never seeing him again. And she had chosen the latter.

He rose and bowed over her hand. It was all over. He had to let her go. "I'm sorry to have given you any distress. I understand your decision, and I am willing to support you in it wholeheartedly." He meant it, but he could feel his smile growing stiff. "I hope you know you are welcome in Cambridge any time."

"Thank you, Jordan," she said quietly. And she returned his smile with one that looked strangely as though her own heart was breaking as well.

Twenty

Phoebe pulled herself up the stairs by the railing. There was a great deal more packing to be done if she was to be ready and waiting at the Dog and Buck tavern for the post at three. Still, a heaviness in her legs made each step harder than the last.

"Milady, a letter came for you. I didn't want to disturb you before, since you were with Professor DeVaux." Annie followed her up the stairs with the sealed paper. It was obvious from her expression that the whole household knew that DeVaux had called and was agog with curiosity.

Phoebe took the letter and with a strange sense of relief at having something else to think about went upstairs to read it.

She smiled at the scribbled heading. It was from Boxty, now in Greece. He sounded happy, exuberant, free. He wrote pages on the architecture of the place. It was obvious that Professor Hillyard had managed to impart quite a good bit of knowledge during their travels. Joxer was being a bit of a wildman, but Grinny was good fun, and of course all sent their regards.

It was satisfying to hear Boxty so pleased. He had

finally escaped the loving stranglehold of Cambridge and had gotten what he wanted.

She glanced at the clock. Was there time to write him back? Not really. The trunks were still overflowing with clothes that for some reason she'd insisted on packing herself, though Annie was likely a good deal more capable. The room where she'd lived for the last four months didn't look in the least bit packed up. There was a string of dried posies from the various picnics they'd gone on, a book on astronomy she'd bought in a moment of weakness, Caldwell's best academic gown that she'd offered to sew a new collar onto. Pinned to the wall by her dressing table was the drawing Will had made for her, and the two little ink footprints Hillary's baby had stamped out under his mother's tutelage.

No, it didn't look as though she were ready to leave at all.

"Milady"—Annie popped her head in the door—"someone else here to see you. Lady Whitcombe. Shall I tell her you're engaged in packing your things?"

Eleanor? She'd never known Eleanor to leave her enclave in Potton. It must be something momentous. "Bother. This is never going to get done today. Continue without me. Pack it however you like." She swept her hand to encompass the room. "I'm taking everything with me."

She went down the stairs, feeling a strange tightness in her throat. She needed time to think over the peculiar events of this morning. It didn't matter. It would all be over soon. She'd be back in London, and it would all be done. "Eleanor," she said, holding out both her hands to her friend, "how pleasant to see you here. I had no idea you were in town."

Eleanor laughed. "DeVaux convinced me to take Will to see Dr. Stalk again. Though of course the boy is very much better. Even I can see that. The man practically threw us out of his house for taking up his time with such a healthy boy. Will has gone off boating with Professor Caldwell."

"How nice," said Phoebe, suspecting that this was the heart of the issue. "Caldwell has always been very fond of Will."

"Indeed. He's very kind." There was a strange tense pause. Eleanor pressed her gloves so tightly together that the leather gave a protesting squeak. "Very kind," she said again.

She'd seen it of course, how Eleanor and Caldwell looked at each other. "Are you fond of him, Eleanor?" she asked gently.

"Yes," came the reluctant reply.

"And he is obviously attached to you. What is the impediment?"

Eleanor looked at her as though she were hopelessly naïve. "Phoebe, I'm notorious. I'm a fallen woman. All the world knows that Will was conceived long after Whitcombe and I began living apart. And they all believe the child to be Jordan DeVaux's. DeVaux and I had talked of marrying, once Whitcombe died . . ."

Phoebe felt a wave of sickness. "Why don't you?"

"If I did it would be a marriage of convenience, you understand. For Will." Eleanor smiled weakly. "The world thinks him Jordan's and this would appear to right a wrong."

"Why don't you?" she asked again, painfully fixing the smile on her face. What right had she to be jealous? She'd told Jordan she wouldn't marry him, hadn't she? Why should she care if he married someone else?

Eleanor opened and closed her hands in her lap, watching them closely as though she'd never seen this trick before. "Because of my feelings for John Caldwell." She forestalled Phoebe's comment with a raised hand. "Oh can't you see it? Estranged wife, scandalous for her affairs, has child by a university professor whom she refuses to marry once her husband conveniently dies, but instead marries his friend."

"I fail to see the problem."

Eleanor threw up her hands. "It would have been so tidy to have married DeVaux. William would have had a father at last, my neighbors would have allowed their children to play with him, and all would be right in society's eyes." She grimaced. "If I married Caldwell, or indeed, if I do not marry at all, society will think me a most shocking creature, and Will . . . Will will have nothing."

She looked up, an angry fire in her eyes. "They tease him already for having two fathers, Whitcombe, and DeVaux. Can you imagine what it would be like if he had three?"

Phoebe sat in silence for a moment, thoughts rushing through her mind like a swollen river. "Do you love Caldwell?" she demanded.

Eleanor looked slightly shocked. "Yes," she answered after a moment. "I do."

Phoebe smiled and sat back on the sofa. "Then your problem is very easily solved. What does it matter what society thinks? Society does not sit down to dinner with you every night. Society does not lie next to you in bed. Don't do what I did. Don't marry because you should. Don't do it because you think you would shock the world if you did not do what they expect. Believe me, all the people you think you will horrify will cease to think of you in a week, no matter what you do to appease them or shock them."

A perverse little voice in Phoebe's head wondered if the opposite was not also true. She had refused Jordan because it all seemed too easy, too right. Was she so determined to flaunt society that she would throw away happiness?

Eleanor was chewing her lip. "Society can go hang. I've shocked them often enough. But Will? How can I deny him a place in well-bred society?"

"Caldwell loves Will. And Caldwell loves you. Are those things not more important than anything else? You can't throw away happiness, particularly some-one else's, just because of something you think should be done."

"Why don't you ask William," she suggested, when Eleanor continued to sit, staring miserably at her hands. "He's a clever boy. He knows what momentous decisions these are."

Eleanor smiled, though Phoebe could see that her thoughts were still undecided. "I have," she admitted. "Will cares nothing about his illegitimacy. And he says he cares nothing for what the other children say. He only wants a father." She laughed her sad little laugh. "DeVaux would have been a good father of course. And DeVaux has always said that he would marry me if I wished it."

Phoebe fought the urgent need to leap to her feet

and shout that Eleanor could marry Caldwell or not as she pleased but that she refused to let her marry DeVaux.

"But Will has told me himself that as long as DeVaux still comes to see him, he can bear the disappointment of not having him as his own papa," Eleanor continued. She looked Phoebe full in the face for the first time. "Would it be very selfish of me to not marry DeVaux in the hopes that things might, perhaps work out with Caldwell?"

Phoebe's heart gave a strange throb and then went still. "No," she said quietly. "I have a feeling it will make a great number of people very happy."

Hillary met Phoebe on the stairs. "Is she gone?" she demanded.

"Lady Whitcombe? Yes. Did you wish to speak with her?"

Hillary wrinkled her nose and looked slightly shamefaced. "No, I just wanted to get a look at her. I've never seen her before. And of course I've heard so much." She drew herself up with dignity. "I'm certain much of it isn't true, of course."

Phoebe smiled. "I'm glad you let me receive her. Many people would not have, and they would have been quite wrong. Lady Whitcombe has suffered a great deal in her life."

Jordan's sister looked slightly mollified. "Well, I'm glad then. But I came to tell you that you must hurry. Hartfield is bringing around the carriage now. If you don't go this instant you will miss the post."

The post. She'd almost forgotten. In another quarter hour she'd be on her way to London.

On her way to her room, she met a caravan of footmen carrying out her trunks. Good heavens, Annie must have worked a miracle. Had it all really gotten packed? She walked into her room and looked around. Gone. It was as prim and empty as it had been when she arrived.

There was nothing left of her life here. Nothing to indicate that she'd been here at all.

She took her spencer from where Annie had left it on the bed and slowly put it on. Downstairs she could hear Hartfield shouting at the footmen as they loaded her trunks.

The pleasure she should have felt in assuring Eleanor's happiness was tempered with a strange feeling of dread. She should be looking forward to going to London. It was what she had wanted all along, was it not? It was what she'd worked so hard for. There was no reason that Jordan's proposal, abrupt and unromantic as it had been, should sway her resolve. As they'd agreed, they'd made their decisions long ago. Just because there was no impediment to their marriage didn't mean that they should marry.

Annie came running into the room. "Milady, Mr. Hartfield says you must come down this minute. You'll be like to miss the post!"

Phoebe looked up, pensive, then shook herself. "Certainly. We'll leave directly." She straightened her shoulders, buttoned her spencer, and followed the maid down the stairs.

Twenty-one

Jordan sat in the observatory at the top of the St. John's College gatehouse and pretended to be studying the star chart pinned to one of the walls. It wouldn't be dark for a long while yet, but he'd needed a safe cave to hide in and this was the one he always seemed to find himself in.

Her coach had been gone for hours. He'd sat here watching the clock, picturing Phoebe standing in the inn yard, waiting for her half-dozen trunks to be loaded onto the coach, imagining the footmen's dismay. He pictured Hillary and Hartfield waving to her as she climbed in. Hartfield would be taciturn as always, and Hillary would be crying and moving the baby's little fist in a goodbye salute. Phoebe herself would hang out the window and wave and smile as long as she could see them. Her affection for them was genuine, despite the fact that she had no desire to live with them forever. And of course that had never been the intention.

He couldn't recall now what the original intention had been, but it didn't seem to matter anymore anyway.

He walked to the slate and began making some calculations. Tonight would be clear, and dark, as fine a night as one could ask for, really, but he could muster little enthusiasm for it.

Phoebe had turned him down. Again. The marvel was really that he'd had the temerity to ask. After that terrible night on the road when he'd discovered her secret, they'd hardly spoken. What would have led him to expect her to fall into his arms and profess her love?

In order to better wallow in self-pity, he tried to remember the days when they'd first met. He recalled them perfectly of course. But strangely, they were like pastoral paintings, pretty and sweet, but with an overblown beauty, an exaggerated utopia. What he missed was the Phoebe he'd gotten to know in Cambridge. The Phoebe who was opinionated, stubborn, wry. The woman who had kissed him with heart-stopping passion in this very room. The woman who knew what she wanted. Even though it wasn't him.

He looked at the clock. She was likely as happy to leave Cambridge as Fuller had been. She was two or three posting houses down the road at least. He was proud of her, in a strange way. She'd wanted to go back to London, and she'd made it happen. The Phoebe he'd known all those years ago wouldn't have done that.

He walked over to the western window and examined the sky. Overhead it was darkening to indigo, at the bottom, still pink and gold. It was a Michelangelo sky, a thousand improbable colors all at once. He watched it, appreciative but removed, and waited for darkness to fall.

Perhaps he'd ask someone to call on her in London. Fuller would do it, of course. Then he'd know if she had found a house that was suitable and if she was economizing too much merely to escape his hateful charity. She would want to know how Hillary and the baby got on, and of course, she'd want news of Will.

He watched the sky darken and drew a painful breath. It had been peaceful here before Phoebe came to Cambridge. He'd been happy in his quiet academic cave. Now, it seemed too quiet.

He heard a familiar tread on the stairs.

"DeVaux!" Caldwell put his head in the door. "I thought I would find you here. You won't be able to see a thing for hours you know."

He shrugged and made a great pretense of writing on the slateboard. "I know. I came up here to think."

Caldwell made a face of disappointment. "Shall I tell her to go away then?"

He whipped around. "Who?"

Under Caldwell's arm he saw a familiar chip bonnet. "Me," said Phoebe. "Only me."

Jordan felt his heart stop and then start pounding abruptly at a runaway clip. "I thought you halfway to London by now," he stammered at last.

Caldwell gave her an encouraging push into the observatory and then closed the door. Jordan resisted the urge to go to her and take her in his arms to be certain she was really there.

She gave him a shy smile. "I was. Or very nearly. Two posting houses down the road I got off."

He stared at her, afraid if he said too much she would go away again. The very last light of the sky touched her cheeks with pink and lit the gold in her hair like a halo. Perhaps she wasn't real after all.

"I walked back," she volunteered.

"Walked?"

She laughed. "Actually a farmer gave Annie and me a ride for most of the way. I've become quite the nipfarthing. You didn't expect me to pay for the hire of a carriage did you?" She walked toward him now and laid a hand on his sleeve. "I needed the time to think."

He held his breath as though she were a butterfly that might flit off with the merest movement. "What were you thinking about, Phoebe?" he asked in a low voice at last.

"I was wondering if there were any falling stars tonight."

Did she know she was beautiful? In the half-light she might have been a dream, but he could feel the light weight of her hand on his arm and smell the scent of her hair. "There are some in the summer. Not so many as during this year's Lyrid's, certainly. But if you wait long enough, you will see one."

A smile curved her lips. "I can wait. I've waited a long time to make this wish; I can wait for a falling star tonight."

He had to ask. "What will you wish for?"

Her eyes were dark in the fading light, but he could see the expression in them. "I wish that you would ask me again to marry you."

His arm stole around her waist. "For the third time? Really, Phoebe, you've grown very excessive."

She frowned, but he saw the dimple beside her mouth. "Do scholars not know the laws of probability?"

He caught her chin in his hand and tilted her face to his. "I'd ask you a thousand times if I thought you would say yes just once."

She looked steadily into his eyes. "It will only take once. I know what I want."

"I love you, Phoebe."

She took him by the lapels and laughed delightedly. "Then marry me. Right away." She rose onto her toes and kissed him. "We'll scandalize the *ton* with our shockingly brief engagement."

All the years of waiting seemed suddenly worth it. He held her in his arms as the stars came out, and they stood in the darkness and whispered their wishes to each other.

The Queen of Romance

Cassie Edwards